Crystal

Crystal

V.C. Andrews®

G.K. Hall & Co. • Chivers Press
Thorndike, Maine USA   Bath, England

This Large Print edition is published by G.K. Hall & Co., USA and by Chivers Press, England.

Published in 1998 in the U.S. by arrangement with Pocket Books, an imprint of Simon & Schuster, Inc.

Published in 1999 in the U.K. by arrangement with Simon & Schuster Ltd.

U.S.   Hardcover   0-7838-0328-1   (Core Series Edition)
U.K.   Hardcover   0-7540-1212-3   (Windsor Large Print)

The text of this Large Print edition is unabridged.
Other aspects of the book may vary from the original edition.

Set in 16pt. Plantin by Al Chase.

Printed in the United States on permanent paper.

British Library Cataloguing in Publication Data available

Library of Congress Cataloging in Publication Data
Andrews, V. C. (Virginia C.)
      Crystal / V. C. Andrews.
         p.   cm.
      ISBN 0-7838-0328-1   (lg. print : hc : alk. paper)
      1. Large type books.   I. Title.
[PS3551.N454C79   1998]
 813'.54—dc21   98-34400

Crystal

Prologue

One night Mr. Philips forgot his keys. It was as simple as that. Even though I was just a little over eleven, I had been helping in the administrative office as usual, filing purchase orders, receipts, and repair orders. I had left Molly Stuart's watch in Mr. Philips's bathroom when I had taken it off to wash my hands. I didn't have a watch, and she let me borrow hers once in a while. When she saw I didn't have it on my wrist, she asked me about it, and I remembered. This was after supper, when we were all in our rooms doing homework. I told her not to worry. I knew where it was. She fumed and fumed until blood flooded her face. She was positive someone would have stolen it by now because Mr. Philips's office door was never locked. So I left my room and hurried downstairs. I entered, put on the lights, and looked in the bathroom. There it was on the sink where I had left it.

I turned to leave, and that was when I saw Mr. Philips's keys on his desk. I knew they were the keys to the secret files, the files that held information about each of us. Other kids were always asking me if I had ever seen the files out while I was working there. I never had.

My heart skipped a beat. I looked at the door and back at those magical keys. It was close to impossible for an orphan to learn about his or her biological past, at least until he or she turned eighteen. All I had ever been told was that my mother had been too sick to keep me and that I had no father.

I had never done a dishonest thing in my life, but this was different, I thought. This was not stealing. This was merely taking something that really belonged to me: knowledge about my own past. Quietly, I closed the front door, and then I went to the desk, picked up the keys, and found the one that would open the drawers containing the secret files.

Funny, how I stood there, afraid to touch the file that had my name on its tab. Was I afraid to break a rule or afraid to learn about myself? Finally, I got up enough nerve and pulled out my file. It was thicker than I had imagined it could be. I turned off the office lights so I wouldn't attract any attention and sat on the floor by the bathroom with the door only slightly ajar. A thin shaft of light escaped and provided enough illumination for me to read the pages.

The first few were filled with information I already knew about myself: medical history, school records. But the bottom stack of pages opened the dark doors of my past and revealed information that both surprised and frightened me.

According to what I read, my mother, Amanda Perry, had been diagnosed as a manic-depressive when she was only in her mid-teens. She was institutionalized at seventeen after repeated efforts to commit suicide, once cutting her wrists and twice trying to overdose with sleeping pills.

I read on and learned that while my mother was in a mental facility, she was impregnated by an attendant. Apparently, they never knew which attendant, so I realized that some degenerate out there was my father, unless I wanted to believe that my mother and this attendant had the most romantic and wonderful love affair between her drug therapies, cold baths, and electric shock treatments.

Anyway, when they realized my mother was pregnant, someone made the official decision not to abort me. After I was born, obviously neither my paternal nor my maternal grandparents wanted anything to do with me, and Mr. Degenerate Attendant wasn't going to come out and claim me, so I was immediately made a ward of the state. My reports didn't say who had named me Crystal. I like to think it was the one and only thing my poor mother had been able to give me. I had nothing else, not even the slightest idea who I was, until I managed to sneak into these files.

I saw a simple statement about my mother's death at the age of twenty-two. Her last attempt at taking her own life was a successful one. I would never meet her, even years from now when I was on my own.

I remember the revelations made my hands shake and gave me a hollow feeling at the base of my stomach. Would I inherit my mother's mental problems? Would I inherit my father's evil ways? After I put the file back, locked up the cabinet, returned the keys to the desk, and left, I had to go right to the bathroom because I felt as if I had to throw up.

I managed to keep my supper down but washed my face with cold water just to calm myself. When I looked in the mirror then, I studied myself, searching my eyes, my mouth, looking for some sign of evil. I felt like Dr. Jekyll searching for a glimpse of Mr. Hyde. From that day forward, I've had nightmares about it. In them I see myself become mentally ill and so sick that I would be put in some clinic and locked away forever.

I suppose it was just natural that any psychologist who knew about my past would wonder if I shared any characteristics with my parents. From what I had read, I understood that my mother apparently acted out in school often and was a very difficult student for all the teachers. She was constantly in trouble. I've never been like that, but I recently read that this sort of behavior is considered a call for help, just as attempting suicide is.

With all these calls for help, the world seemed like a great big ocean with many people drowning and lifeguards whimsically choosing to help this one or that one. Naturally, the richer ones always were saved or at least tossed a lifeline. Those like me were shoved into mental institutions, group foster homes, orphanages, and prisons. We were swept under the rug with so many others. It made me wonder how anyone could walk on it.

I never told anyone what I had learned, of course, but I began to understand why it was that few prospective parents ever showed interest in me. They probably were given information about my past and decided not to take a chance on someone like me.

Once, when I was at a different orphanage, I was sitting outside and reading *The Diary of Anne Frank.* (I was always two or three reading grade levels above other kids my age.) Suddenly, I felt a shadow move over me, and I looked up to see a balloon drifting in the wind, the string dangling like a tail. Some little child had loosened his or her grip, and it had escaped. Now, however, it drifted aimlessly, attached to no one, doomed never to return to its owner. It disappeared over a rim of treetops, and I thought, that's what we're all like here, balloons that someone released willingly or unwillingly, poor souls lost and sailing into the wind, waiting and hoping for another hand to take hold of us and bring us back to earth.

Three more years went by without my being adopted or given a foster home. I was still helping Mr. Philips in his office, and about a year ago, he started calling me Little Miss Efficiency. I didn't mind it, even when he used me to rankle his assistants. He always said things like, "Why can't you be as responsible or as careful as Crystal?" He even said that occasionally to his secretary, Mrs. Mills.

Mrs. Mills always looked as if she were drowning in carbon copies. Her fingers were usually blue or black because of ribbons, ink cartridges, and toner she had to change. In the morning, she came to work looking as well put together as a work of classical art, not a strand of her blue-gray hair out of place, her makeup perfect, her clothing clean and unwrinkled, but by the end of the day, her bangs were always dangling over her eyes, her blouse usually had a smudge somewhere on it, maybe two, her lipstick had somehow spread onto a cheek, and she had become a work of abstract art. I know she's one person who never resented me. She was always happy to greet me and appreciated the work I did, work she would probably have had to do otherwise.

For someone my age, I know a lot about human psychology. I got interested in it after I read about my mother. Now I'm thinking I might be a doctor someday, and anyway, it's good to know as much as you can about psychology. It comes in handy, especially around orphanages.

But it's not always an asset to be smarter than other people or more responsible. This is especially true for orphans. The more helpless you seem, the better your chances are for being adopted. If you look as if you can take care of yourself, who wants you? At least, that's another one of my theories for why I was a prisoner of the system for as long as I was. Prospective adoption parents don't like feeling inferior to the child they might adopt. I've seen it firsthand.

There was this couple who asked specifically for me. They wanted a child who was older. The woman, whose name was Chastity, had a silly little grin on her face. Her husband called her Chas, and she called him Arn, short for Arnold. I suppose they would have ended up calling me Crys. Completing words was difficult for them. They had the same problem with sentences, always leaving a part dangling, like when Chas asked me, "What do you want to be when you . . ."

"When I what?" I forced her to say.

"Get older. Graduate from . . ."

"College or high school or the armed services or secretarial school or computer training?" I cataloged. I had taken an immediate dislike to them. She giggled too much, and he looked as if he wanted to be someplace else the moment he walked into the room.

"Yes," she said, giggling.

"I suppose I want to be a doctor, but I might want to be a writer. I'm not absolutely sure. What do you want to be?" I asked her, and she batted her eyelashes with a smile of utter confusion.

"What?"

"When you . . ." I looked at Arn, and he smirked.

Her smile wilted like a flower and gradually evaporated completely. Her eyes were forbidding and soon filled with a nervous energy. I couldn't count how many times she gazed longingly at the door.

They looked quite relieved when the interview ended. I didn't have another interview until just a week ago, but I was happy to met Thelma and Karl Morris. Apparently, my background didn't frighten them, nor did my being precocious annoy them. In fact, afterward, Mr. Philips told me I was exactly what they wanted: an adolescent who promised to be no problem, who wouldn't make a major demand on their lives, who had some independence, and who was in good health.

Thelma seemed convinced that whatever damage she believed I'd suffered as an orphan would be corrected after a few weeks of life in her and Karl's home. I loved her cockeyed optimism. She was a small woman in her late twenties with very curly light brown hair and hazel eyes that were as bright and innocent as a six-year-old's.

Karl was only a few inches taller, with thin dark brown hair and dull brown eyes. He looked much older but was only in his early thirties. He had a soft, friendly smile that settled in his pudgy face like berries in cream. He was stout. His hands were small, but his fingers were thick.

He was an accountant, and she said she was a housewife, but they had long ago decided that was a job, too, and she should be paid a salary for it. She had even gotten raises when they had good years. They couldn't stop talking about themselves. It was as if they wanted to get out their entire lives in one meeting.

The best thing I could say about them was that there was absolutely nothing subtle, contrived, or threatening about them. What you saw was what you got. I liked that. It made me feel at ease. At times during the interview, it was more as if I was there to decide if *I* would adopt *them*.

"Everything is just too serious here," Thelma told me toward the end of our session. She grimaced, folding her mouth into a disapproving frown. "It's just too serious a place for a young person to think of as any sort of home. I don't hear any laughter. I don't see any smiles."

Then she suddenly grew very serious herself and leaned toward me to whisper. "You don't have a boyfriend yet, do you? I'd hate to break up a budding romance."

"Hardly," I told her. "Most of the boys

here are quite immature." She liked that and was immediately relieved.

"Good," she said. "Then it's settled. You'll come home with us, and we'll never speak of anything unpleasant again. We don't believe in sadness — if you don't think about the bad things in life, you'll find they all just go away. You'll see."

I should have known what that meant, but for once in my short life, I decided to stop analyzing everyone and just enjoy the company of someone, especially someone who wanted to be my mother.

1

A New Beginning

🍃

Going home with the Morrises was like taking a guided tour of their lives on a sightseeing bus. They drove a moderately priced sedan chosen, Karl said, for its gas efficiency and for its high rating in *Consumer Reports*.

"Karl makes the decisions about everything we buy," Thelma explained with a light laugh that punctuated most of what she said. "He says an informed consumer is a protected consumer. You can't believe in advertisements. Advertisements, especially commercials, are just full of a lot of misinformation, right, Karl?"

"Yes, dear," Karl agreed.

I sat in the rear, and Thelma remained turned on an angle so she could talk to me all the way to their home — my new home — in Wappingers Falls, New York.

"Karl and I were childhood sweethearts. Did I tell you that?"

She continued before I could tell her she had.

"We started to go together in the tenth

grade, and when Karl went to college, I remained faithful to him, and he remained faithful to me. After he graduated and was appointed to his position at IBM, we planned our wedding. Karl helped my parents make all the arrangements, right down to the best place to go for flowers, right, Karl?"

"That's true," he said, nodding. He didn't take his eyes off the road.

"Ordinarily, Karl doesn't like to have long conversations in the car when he's driving," Thelma explained, gazing at him and smiling. "He says people forget how driving a car is something that requires their full attention."

"Especially nowadays," Karl elaborated, "with so many more cars on the road, so many more teenage drivers and older drivers. Those two age groups account for more than sixty percent of all accidents."

"Karl has all sorts of statistics like that floating around his mind," Thelma said proudly. "Just last week, I was thinking about replacing our gas stove with a new electric range, and Karl converted BTUs . . . is that it, Karl? BTUs?"

"Yes."

"BTUs into pennies of cost and showed me how the gas stove was more efficient.

Isn't it wonderful to have a husband like Karl who can keep you from making the wrong decisions?"

I smiled and gazed out the windows. The orphanage wasn't much more than fifty or so miles from where my new parents lived, but I had never traveled this far north. Other than some school field trips, I hadn't been to many places at all. Just leaving the orphanage and going twenty miles by car was an adventure.

It was late summer, and the cooler autumn winds had already begun to descend from the north. Leaves were turning rust and orange, and when I could see far into the distance and look over the heavily wooded mountains, I thought the ripple of colors was breathtakingly beautiful. This was a bright, sunny day, too. The sky was a deep, rich blue, and the clouds that flowed across it in a stream of wind stretched themselves until they became as thin as gauze. Way off to the south, an airplane turned into a silver dot and then disappeared into the clouds.

I was happy and full of hope. I would have a home, a place to call my own, and someone else to care about besides myself, as well as, I hoped, someone to care about me. How simple that was and how taken for granted by most people, but how wonderful and new and precious it was for orphans like myself.

"Karl is the oldest of three brothers and the only one married. His middle brother, Stuart, is a salesman for an air-conditioner manufacturer in Albany, and his younger brother, Gary, has graduated from a culinary institute in Poughkeepsie, where Karl's father lives. Gary was hired to cook on a cruise ship, so we don't hear from him or see him much at all.

"Karl and his brothers are not far apart in age, but they're not all that close. No one is in Karl's family, right, Karl?"

Karl nearly turned to look at her. His head started to move and then stopped when an automobile about fifty yards in front of us emerged from a driveway and he had to slow down.

"If they didn't speak to each other on the phone occasionally, they wouldn't know who still existed in the family and who didn't. Karl's father is still alive, but his mother passed away, what, two years ago, Karl?"

"A year and eleven months tomorrow," Karl said mechanically.

"A year and eleven months," she repeated like a translator.

So I have two uncles and a grandfather on Karl's side, I thought. Before I could ask about her side, she volunteered the information.

"I don't have any brothers or sisters," Thelma said. "My mother wasn't supposed to have any children. She had breast cancer when she was only seventeen, and the doctors advised her not to have children. Then, late in life, when she was in her early thirties, she became pregnant with me. My father was forty-one at the time. Now my mother is fifty-eight and my father is sixty-nine.

"I bet you're wondering why we don't have any children of our own. Before you, I mean," she added quickly.

"It's none of my business," I said.

"Oh, sure it is. Everything that's our business is your business now. We're going to be a family, so we have to share and be honest with each other, right, Karl?"

"Absolutely," he said, signaling to change lanes and pass the car ahead of us.

"Karl's sperm count is too low," she said with a smile, as if she were delighted about it.

"I don't know if we should talk about *that*, Thelma." The back of Karl's neck turned pink with embarrassment.

"Oh, of course we can. She's old enough and probably knows everything there is to know. Kids today are very advanced. How can they not help it, with all that's on television? Do you watch television much, Crystal?"

"No," I answered.

"Oh," she said, the excitement fading in her face for the first time since we had met. Her eyes looked like tiny flashlights with weakened batteries. Then she thought of something and smiled again. "Well, that's probably because you didn't have much opportunity in a home with so many other children. Anyway, we did try to have children. As soon as Karl determined it was financially sensible for us, we tried, right, Karl?"

He nodded.

"Nothing happened no matter how we planned it. I used a thermometer to take my temperature, plotted the days on my calendar, even planned some romantic evenings," she said, blushing. She shrugged. "Nothing happened. We just thought we were missing," she continued. "Take better aim, I used to tell him, didn't I, Karl?"

"Thelma, you're embarrassing me," he said.

"Oh, fiddledy-doo. We're a family. We can't be embarrassed," she emphasized.

The simplicity and honesty with which she talked about the most intimate details of her life fascinated me.

"Anyway," she continued, turning back to

me, "Karl read up on it and learned that he should keep his scrotum cool. He avoided wearing anything tight, refrained from taking hot baths, and tried to keep himself cool, especially before we were going to make a baby. We even waited longer between times because periods of sexual restraint usually increase the volume and potency of sperm, right, Karl?"

"You don't have to get into the nitty-gritty details, Thelma."

"Oh, sure I do. I want Crystal to understand. I was reading a magazine the other day, *Modern Parent* or something like that, and the article said mothers and daughters especially should be honest and open about everything so they can build trust.

"Where was I?" she asked. "Oh, volume and potency of sperm. So, when that didn't work, we went to a doctor. You know that the average male produces anywhere from 120 million to 600 million sperm in a single ejaculation?"

"You have trouble with so many other facts and statistics, Thelma. How come you don't forget that one?" Karl asked gently.

"I don't know. It's not easy to forget, I guess," she said, shrugging. "Anyway, we found out that Karl was way below that and it didn't matter what he did. We still tried

24

and tried, of course, and then we finally decided to adopt. Actually, I got the idea from *Throbs of the Heart* by Torch Summers, and then I discussed it with Karl and he agreed it would be a good idea.

"However, taking care of a baby is not an easy job. You have to wake up at night, and then you're too tired to do anything the next day, even watch television. So, that's how come we went looking for an older child and found you," she concluded.

"Our baby-making problem is not that unusual," Karl interjected during the first quiet moment. "Infertility used to be thought mainly a woman's problem, but the problem lies with the man in thirty-five percent of the cases."

"Karl feels sorry, but I don't blame him," Thelma said in a voice a little above a whisper. "It's like what happens in *Love's Second Chance* by Amanda Fairchild. Did you ever read that one? I know you read a lot."

"No," I said. "I've never heard of it."

"Oh. Well, I think it was number one on the romance chart for four months last year. Anyway, April's lover has Karl's problem, only he doesn't know it until after April gets pregnant, obviously with someone else's child. It's so sad at the end when April dies in childbirth."

Thelma's eyes actually teared over. Then she jumped in her seat and smiled.

"Let's not think of sad things today. To-day's a big day for all of us. We're going to a restaurant for dinner tonight, right, Karl?"

"Yes. I thought we'd go to the Sea Shell. Do you like seafood, Crystal?" he asked.

"I haven't eaten much of it, but yes," I said.

"Ordinarily, we don't go out to eat. It's not practical," Thelma said. "But Karl be-lieves the Sea Shell gives you the best value for your dollar."

"Lobster and shrimp are expensive in res-taurants especially, but they give you a good combination plate and plenty of salad and bread. I like their combination dinners. Good value," he pointed out. "You'll like their choice of desserts, too. I bet you like chocolate cake."

"It's my favorite," I admitted. All this talk of food was making my stomach growl.

"We have so much to learn about each other," Thelma said. "I want to know all your favorite things, like your favorite colors, favorite movie stars, favorite everything. I hope we have a lot of the same favorites, but even if we don't, it won't matter," she as-sured me, nodding so firmly it looked as if she was assuring herself just as much.

26

A little more than an hour later, we drove up a residential street and pulled into the driveway of a small ranch-style house with light gray aluminum siding, black aluminum window shutters, a sidewalk between two patches of lawn, hedges along the sidewalk and in front of the house, and a red maple tree off to the left. A large, plain aluminum mailbox in front was labeled MORRIS and had the address printed under it.

"Home sweet home," Thelma said as the garage door went up.

We pulled into the garage, a garage that looked neater than some of the rooms in the orphanage. It had shelves on the rear wall, and everything on them was labeled and organized. The floor of the garage even had a carpet over it.

Karl helped with my luggage and my box of books. I followed them through a door that led right into the kitchen.

"Karl designed our house," Thelma explained. "He thought it was practical to come directly from the garage into the kitchen, so we could get our groceries easily out of the car and into their proper cabinets."

It was a small but very neat and clean-looking kitchen. There was a breakfast nook on the right with a bay window that looked out on a fenced-in backyard. There wasn't much more lawn in the rear of the house than there was in the front.

Above the table was a cork board with notes pinned to it and a calendar with dates circled. The front of the refrigerator had a magnetic board with a list of foods that had to be replaced.

"Right this way," Karl said.

We left the kitchen and walked through a small corridor that led first to the living room and front door. There was a short entryway with a closet for coats just inside it. There was a den off the entryway that had walls of bookcases, sofas, and chairs, all facing the large television set. Just past that was the dining room. The furniture was all colonial.

My room wasn't much larger than my room at the orphanage, but it had bright, flowery wallpaper, filmy white cotton curtains, a desk with a large cupboard above it, and a twin-size bed with pink and white pillows and comforter. There was a closet on the left and a smaller one on the right.

"You can use this smaller closet for storing things other than clothes," Karl explained.

I paused at the desk and opened the cupboard to see a computer all set up inside.

"Surprise!" Thelma cried, clapping. "We

got that just for you only two days ago. Karl priced them and found the best deal."

"It's very updated," Karl said. "I have you connected to the Internet also, so you can get your research done right in your room when you start school in a few weeks."

"Thank you," I said, overwhelmed. No one had ever bought me anything expensive. For a moment, it took my breath away, and I just ran the tips of my fingers over the keys to check that it was real.

"Now, don't you get like some of those other children we hear about," Thelma warned, "and spend all your time alone staring at the computer screen. We want to be a family and spend time together at dinner and watching television."

"Me, too," I said, nodding. I was really too excited to listen to anything she said. "Thank you."

"It's our pleasure," Karl said.

"I'll help you unpack your clothes, and we'll see what new things you'll need right away. We'll make a list, and Karl will tell us where it's best to go, right, Karl?"

"Absolutely," he said.

"Oh, dear. Oh, dear, no!" Thelma said, suddenly putting her hand to her heart.

Mine skipped a beat. Had I done something wrong already?

29

"What's the matter?" Karl asked her.

"Look at the time," she said, nodding at the small clock on my computer desk. "It's a little past three. I'm missing *Hearts and Flowers*, and today Ariel learns if Todd is the father of her child. Do you watch that one?" she asked me. I looked at Karl for help. I had no idea what she was talking about.

"She means her soap opera. How can she follow that one, Thelma? She would probably be coming home from school or still be in school when that one is on."

"Oh, I forgot that. Well, you know what I do when I have to miss a show. I videotape it. Only, with all the excitement, I forgot to set up the videotape machine. Do you mind waiting a little, dear? I'll help you unpack as soon as the show's over."

"That's all right," I said, putting my first suitcase on the bed and snapping it open. "There isn't much for me to do."

"No, no, no, Crystal, sweetheart." She reached for my hand. "You come with me. We'll watch the show together," she said, "and then we'll take care of your room."

I glanced at Karl, hoping he would rescue me as Thelma pulled me toward the door.

"Thelma, remember we have to get ready precisely at five to go to the restaurant," he said.

"Okay, Karl," she said. She was really tugging me. I practically flew out of the room.

"Welcome to our happy home," Karl called after me.

2
Another World

One of the biggest fears any of us orphans has is that when we do become part of a family, we won't be able to adjust to their style of life. We won't know how to behave at their dinner table, how to behave in front of the other relatives, how to keep our rooms and spend our time. In short, we won't know how to please our new parents. For us it would always be like an audition. We'd feel their eyes following us everywhere we went, hear their whispers, wonder what they really thought. Were they happy they had taken us into their lives, or were they sorry and looking for a graceful way to give us back?

It was easy to adapt to life with my new parents, to know what they expected, liked, and disliked. There was nothing unpredictable about Karl. He was the most organized person I had ever met. He rose at precisely the same time every day, weekend or not.

"People make a mistake sleeping later on the weekends," he told me. "It confuses their body clock."

He also ate the same thing for breakfast every weekday, a combination of cold cereals, mixing the correct formula of fibers and grains with fruit. On weekends, he made himself an omelet with egg whites, or he had oatmeal and raisins. Although he was chubby, he paid attention to nutrition and wanted me to do the same.

What he didn't do was exercise. He admitted that this was a fault, but he made little effort to correct it, the closest thing being his purchase of a treadmill, after what he described as months and months of comparison shopping. I commented that it looked brand new, and he confessed that he still had to develop a regular schedule for its use.

"Maybe now that you're here to remind me," he said, "I'll pay more attention to those things."

I didn't think he needed my reminders for anything. All of his things were organized and inventoried. He knew exactly how many socks he had, how many white shirts, how many pairs of pants and jackets, how many ties. He could even tell me how much each item had cost. What was even more impressive was he knew just how many times he had worn what and knew when something had to be cleaned and pressed. He serviced his clothes the way people service their cars, and when something had been worn, cleaned, or washed a certain number of times, he retired it to a bag marked "To be donated."

Karl continued his organized, regimented existence throughout his day, always eating at the same hour in the evening, watching his news program, reading his newspapers and his magazines, and going to sleep at exactly ten P.M. every night, even on weekends, unless they had plans for an evening out.

If Thelma indicated she wanted to see a movie, Karl would research the reviews and report to her first, deciding whether or not it was a waste of money. If there was any doubt, he would suggest the matinee show because it was discounted and wasn't as great a risk.

"Balance, Crystal," he explained. "That's what makes life truly comfortable, maintaining balance. Assets on one side, liabilities on the other. Everything you do, everyone you meet has assets and liabilities. Learn what they are, and you'll know how to proceed."

He often lectured to me like that, and I listened respectfully, even though many times I thought he was being obsessive about it. Not everything in life could be measured on a profit-and-loss statement, I thought.

In a way, Thelma's life was almost as regimented and organized as Karl's, only hers was determined by the television scheduling of her soap operas and other programs. If she left the house for any reason during the day, she scheduled her appointments and errands around what was on TV that day. Although she could videotape shows, she said it wasn't the same as being there when they were actually on.

"It's like watching history being made rather than watching it later on the news," she told me.

She had reading time reserved, as well, and sat on her rocker with a lace shawl around her shoulders, reading whatever had come in that month from her romance novels club. Pots could boil over, phones could ring, someone might come to the door. It didn't matter once she was engrossed in her story; she didn't care. She truly left one world for another.

Nevertheless, she was as devoted to Karl and his needs as any wife could be. On Sundays, Karl would plan the week's menu, carefully selecting foods that could be utilized in different ways so as to justify buying them in larger quantities or make use of leftovers. Thelma would then develop that menu, following it to a T. If something wasn't just the way Karl had planned it, she treated it like a major crisis. One morning, I had to go with her to another supermarket nearly twenty miles away because the one she shopped at didn't have the brand of canned peaches Karl wanted.

Whereas Karl was a quiet, careful driver, Thelma talked so much from the moment she sat behind the wheel that my ears were ringing. Her attention was often distracted, and twice I jumped so high I nearly bumped my head on the roof when she crossed lanes abruptly and drivers honked their horns.

A week after I arrived, we took a ride to visit Karl's father. He lived alone in a small Cape Cod–style house, the same house he had lived in for nearly forty years. It was in a very quiet, old residential neighborhood of single-family homes, most as old as Karl's father's.

Karl's father was taller and considerably thinner than his son, with a face that reminded me of Abraham Lincoln, long and chiseled. From the pictures I saw on the table in the living room, I concluded Karl took after his mother more. His brothers, on the other hand, resembled their father, both being taller and leaner than Karl.

Papa Morris, as he was introduced to me, was a feisty old man who had worked for the city water department. He was content to live on his pension and social security, socialize with his retired friends, play cards, visit the local bar, and read his newspapers. Karl had arranged for a woman to come and clean twice a week, but Karl's father wouldn't permit anyone to cook for him.

"When I can't take care of myself, I'll know it," he muttered after Karl had made the suggestion again.

However, the kitchen wasn't very clean. Pots were caked with beans and rice, and some dishes were piled up, waiting for the cleaning lady. Thelma went right to work when we arrived. I helped her, and we got the kitchen into some order while Karl and his father talked. Then we all sat in the living room and had fresh lemonade.

Papa Morris stared at me with interest while Thelma described what a wonderful beginning we had all had together since I had come to live with her and Karl. Papa Morris's large, glassy brown eyes narrowed with suspicion.

"You like livin' with these two?" he asked me skeptically.

"Yes, sir," I answered quickly.

"Yes, sir?" he muttered, and looked at Karl, who sat with his hands in his lap.

"She's a very polite young lady," Thelma said. "A lot like Whelma Matthews on *Days in the Sun*," she added, looking at me proudly.

"You don't have to call me sir, Missy. No one's ever called me sir. I don't wear no airs. I'm just a pensioner."

"She's very smart, Pa. All A's in school," Thelma continued.

"That's good." He nodded at me, his face softening some. "My Lily always wanted grandchildren, but none of my boys gave her any. Grandchildren are sort of a return on your investment," he muttered.

"Speaking of investments," he continued, turning to Karl, "what's been happening with that mutual fund you had me put my CD into, Karl?"

"You're up twenty-two percent, Dad."

"Good. Smart boy, Karl," he said, and reached into his top pocket for some chewing tobacco.

"You should give that up, Dad. It's been known to cause mouth cancer," Karl said. "I was just reading an article about that yesterday."

"I've been doing it for fifty years. No point in stopping something I enjoy now, right, Thelma?"

She looked at Karl apprehensively. "Well, I . . ."

"Of course you should, and of course

there's a point to stopping, Dad. Why cause yourself unnecessary suffering?" Karl insisted.

"I'm not suffering. I'm enjoying. I don't know who's a worse nag, you or that woman you send around here. All she does is complain about the work I make for her. How much you paying her?"

"Ten dollars an hour," Karl said.

"Ten dollars! You know," he said, looking at me, "once that was enough to feed the family for a week."

"There have been many reasons for inflation since then," I said.

"That so? You an economic genius like Karl?" he asked me.

"No, sir. I just read a little."

"Oh, she reads a lot, Pa. She reads more than I do," Thelma said.

"Lily liked to read," he said, and thought a moment. Then he slapped his hand down hard on the arm of his chair. Thelma and I jumped in our seats.

"Well now, you bring this polite young lady around more often," he said, rising.

"We can stay a little longer, Pa," Thelma said.

"Well, I can't," he said. "I've got to meet Charlie, Richard, and Marty at Gordon's for our regular game of pinochle," he told her sternly.

Thelma looked to Karl.

"Well, we just came by to introduce you to Crystal and see how you were doing, Dad," Karl said, standing.

"I'm doing as good as I can with what I got," he said, looking toward me.

We all rose.

"Pleased to have met you," he said to me. He held out his hand, and I shook it. He had long, rough fingers with fingernails that were yellow and thick and two years past when they should have been trimmed.

On the way home, I thought about him and about what I'd always imagined my grandparents to be like. Never in any of my dreams did I imagine myself shaking hands with them. I thought they would be full of hugs and kisses, gloating over me and bragging about me just the way they did in movies and books. Maybe Thelma's mother and father would be more like that, I hoped.

And they were.

Thelma's mother was a small woman like her, actually smaller, birdlike and very thin with wrists that looked as if they might crack if she lifted a full cup of coffee, but she had a big smile and the loveliest blue-green eyes. She kept her hair its natural gray and styled neatly. Thelma's father was tall and lean but much warmer than Karl's father. They insisted I call them Grandpa and Grandma immediately, and Grandma hugged and kissed me as soon as we were all introduced.

"I'm so happy there'll be someone young in this house. Now it will be a real home. You make sure you spoil this child, Karl Morris," she warned, shaking her right forefinger in his face. "None of that thinking like an accountant when it comes to her. That's what parents are supposed to do, and if you don't, we will," she added with a mock threat.

Before they left that day, they even gave me twenty dollars. Grandma said, "Buy whatever Karl doesn't want you to have, whatever he thinks is a waste of money." She laughed and kissed me again. I liked her a lot and looked forward to the next time I would see her.

Of all that had happened since I had come to live with Karl and Thelma, this was the best, I thought. My grandparents had finally made me feel part of a real family. Life with Karl and Thelma had started on such a formal and organized note, I had yet to think of them as parents. Karl was more like an adviser, and Thelma was so wrapped up in her books and programs that I felt more like a guest she had invited to share her fantasies.

I was looking forward to the start of

school, making new friends, and being chal-
lenged by new subjects and teachers.
Thelma took me to registration. Because of
my record, I was put in an advanced class,
and she bragged about it all throughout dinner that night. As always, however, she
found a fictional character with whom to
compare me.

"Brenda's daughter in *Thunder in My
Heart* is just like you, Crystal. She's such a
whiz kid, too. Maybe she'll be president
someday."

"How can Brenda's daughter be president
someday, Thelma?" Karl asked her. "She's
in a book you've read, right?"

"Oh, but there's a sequel coming, Karl.
There's always a sequel," she said, smiling.

"I see," he said, nodding and looking at
me.

"Crystal's smarter, though," Thelma said.
"You should hear some of the things she
says, Karl. She can figure out what's going to
happen on my soaps before it happens."

"They're pretty predictable," I commented.

"What's that mean?" Thelma asked, bat-
ting her eyelashes.

"It means they're not hard to figure out,"
Karl said. "They're simple."

"Oh." She laughed her thin laugh.

"They're hard for me," she said.

Karl gazed at me, and we talked about something else. I felt bad about it and afterward apologized.

"I didn't mean to make fun of your programs, Thelma," I said.

"Oh, did you make fun of them? I didn't think you did. How could you make fun of them? They're so full of excitement and romance. Don't you like that?"

"I like good stories, yes," I said.

"There, then. I knew you would. Don't forget, tomorrow we'll learn about November's ex-husband. Do you think he still loves her?"

"I don't remember him," I admitted. She looked at me as if I had said the silliest thing.

"You can't forget Edmond. He's soooo handsome. If he came to my front door, I'd swoon," she told me, following with her little, thin laugh.

I wondered if everyone who watched soap operas was as committed to them and as involved with them as Thelma was. A few days later, one of her favorite characters died on *Days in the Sun*. I came in on the show just as it happened, and she began to sob so hard, I got frightened. She started to shout at the television set.

"He can't be dead. He can't be. How can

he die? Please don't let him die. Oh, Crystal, he's dead! Grant's dead! How can he be dead?"

"People die in real life, Mom," I said, "so they have to have some die in the shows, don't they?"

"No," she insisted, her face filled with more anger than I had seen up until now. "It's not fair. They got us to love him, and now they've killed him. It's not fair!" she cried.

She went into a deep depression afterward, and nothing I could say or do changed it. She was still that way when Karl came home and we all sat down to dinner. He asked why she was so sad, and she told him and then burst into tears again. He looked at me, and I looked down at my plate. My heart was thumping. I didn't know what to say.

"You're frightening your daughter," Karl remarked.

She looked at me and swallowed back her sobs.

"Oh. I didn't mean to frighten you, Crystal. It's just so sad."

"It's only a show, Mom," I said. "Tomorrow, something new will happen, and you'll feel better."

"Yes, yes, I will. That's right. See Karl, see

·how smart she is?"

"That I do," Karl said.

We finished our meal, but afterward, I found Thelma in her rocker just staring at the floor.

"I'm going upstairs to read and sleep now," I said.

"What? Oh, yes, good night, dear. Try to think good thoughts. Poor Grant," she said. "It makes me think of how it was when Karl's mother died."

I stared at her. How could the death of a real person be the same as the death of a soap opera character?

"He's an actor, Mom. He'll be back on another show," I said softly.

"Who is?"

"Grant."

"No, silly," she said. "Grant's not an actor. Grant was a person who died. I don't think of them as actors," she admitted. She started rocking again and stared at the floor. "Everyone will be so sad tomorrow on the show, so sad."

"Maybe you shouldn't watch it, then," I suggested. She looked up at me as if what I had said was blasphemous.

"I've got to watch it, Crystal. I care about them all. They're my friends," she said. She made it seem as if they knew she was watching and they depended on her.

She looked at the floor again instead of kissing me good night as she had done from the first day I had arrived. I hurried upstairs to sleep. I didn't know exactly why, but for the first time since I had come to live there, I felt a little trepidation. I lay there wondering why. I guess I was afraid that my new mother would always care more about her characters than she would about me.

I had found a home full of family pictures, talk about relatives, promises for upcoming holidays and trips. I had grandparents, and I would soon be in a new school. I had my own room, and I had begun a whole new life.

But what if I woke up in the morning and found that someone had turned a dial and I was back in the orphanage?

3
Peas in a Pod
🍂

Two days before school began, I was sitting outside and reading. Thelma wanted me to watch *Emergency Care* with her. It was a new late-morning series about an ER at a big-city hospital. She tried to get me to watch it with her by telling me I would learn a lot of medical information.

"And you do think you want to be a doctor someday, Crystal," she emphasized. "So you'll learn a lot."

"I'll learn more from reading," I told her. I saw it made her unhappy, but I felt as if I was overdosed on soap operas and television in general. At the orphanage, if I watched two shows a week, that was a lot. I knew most of the other kids my age thought I was weird because I'd rather read a book or work on the computer than watch their favorite nighttime shows, but that's how I was.

It was also a beautiful day, and I couldn't see myself wasting it closed up in the living room with the glow of a television screen on my eyes. This was actually my favorite time of the year. Summer was fading fast, and the air had the feel of the soon-to-be crisp autumn days. It smelled fresher, looked clearer. Without the humidity and high temperatures, I felt more energetic. I was even restless sitting and reading.

"Hi," I heard someone say, and looked up to see a girl about my age with long, sunflower-yellow hair standing at our front gate. She wore a pair of baggy shorts and a T-shirt with half moons all over it. A pair of long silver earrings with tiny blue and green stones dangled from her ears. "I live over there," she said, pointing to a house across the street.

"Hi," I said, and tried to remember if I'd seen her around the neighborhood.

"You just moved in with Karl and Thelma, right? I heard about it," she said before I could respond. She tossed some strands of her hair back over her shoulder as if she were tossing away a candy wrapper. "My name's Helga. I think we're going to be in the same class. You're going into tenth?"

"Yes. I'm Crystal," I said.

"Helga and Crystal. They'll think we're sisters." She giggled. She put all her weight on her right leg. From where I was sitting, it looked as if she was leaning against an imaginary wall. "What are you reading?"

"*Lord of the Flies.* It's on our English reading list this year," I said.

"How do you know that?"

"I asked when I registered, and they gave me the list," I told her.

She grimaced, bounced her weight to her left leg and then back to her right, which I would discover later was something she habitually did when she was confused or annoyed.

"You're doing schoolwork already?" she whined.

"Why not?" I shrugged. "I like being ahead."

"You must be a good student," she said, lingering at the gate. She sounded disappointed.

"Aren't you?" I asked.

She shrugged.

"I get C's and sometimes B's. As long as I don't get D's and F's, my parents don't bug me. Did you live with some other family last year?" she followed quickly.

"No," I said.

She stared at me as if she was building the courage to ask another question.

"I lived in an orphanage," I explained.

"Oh. Did you have any brothers or sisters you had to leave behind or who got adopted into other families?"

"No," I said, "but I've seen that happen, and it's not pleasant."

She smiled. "I hope you don't mind me being nosy. My mother says it's a family character trait. As soon as we hear or see something that's not really our business, we perk up and stick our ears out. She says our family was the inspiration for the first spies."

I laughed.

"You want to go for a walk? I'll show you the neighborhood," she said.

"Okay," I said, standing. I paused for a moment and looked back at the front door.

"What's wrong?" she asked.

"I'm just wondering if I should tell my mother."

"Your mother? Oh, they make you check in and out?"

"No."

"So? We're just going down the street."

I nodded. Since I didn't expect to be away long, I decided not to interrupt her soap opera.

It wasn't until I walked up to Helga that I realized she was at least three inches taller than I was. She had patches of tiny freckles over the crests of her cheeks, and it looked as if someone had dotted them with a ballpoint pen in light brown ink.

"Those are pretty thick glasses you're

wearing," she said.

"I have a stigmatism."

"Bummer," she said. "You oughtta go with me to the mall one day and get nicer frames. Maybe prescription sunglasses, too. You'll look better."

"I don't wear them for looks. I wear them to help me see and read," I said.

She laughed. "Sure. Until someone like Tom MacNamara looks your way. He's so cool, but he's a senior this year and probably won't even look at us. He also happens to be captain of the football team."

"I probably wouldn't be interested in him anyway," I said, and she stopped walking.

"Sure you wouldn't." She bounced her weight from one leg to the other. "Did you have a boyfriend at the orphanage?"

"No. I have never really had a boyfriend," I admitted.

She stared a moment and then started walking again.

"Me, neither," she confessed. "Oh, I pretended to like Jack Martin one year just so it looked like I had a boyfriend, but I never even kissed him, and when he went to kiss me, I turned my head so he kissed my cheek like an uncle or someone. You see this big house?" she said, pausing. "Clara Seymour lives here. She's a senior this year and will probably be senior prom queen. Her father's a heart doctor, a cardio-something."

"Cardiologist," I said.

"Yes, I think that's it." She tilted her head and squinted at me. "You are smart."

"I'm thinking of becoming a doctor myself someday."

"A doctor!" she said. "It costs a lot, I heard."

"I hope to win scholarships, too," I added.

"I'll be glad just to get my diploma. I haven't the slightest idea what I'll do. I was thinking I might become an actress, but I didn't even make the junior play."

"What do you like to do?"

"Party," she said, laughing, "and watch television. Oh!" She stopped and took my arm. "Watch out for the dog at this house," she said, nodding at a small A-frame. "Old Lady Potter lives there, and she has a mean rottweiler for protection. Last year, he bit a UPS delivery driver and there was a big commotion with the police and everything."

"I'll definitely stay out of that yard." I laughed. "Thanks for the advice."

"If you turn right at the corner and go two blocks, you reach the Quick Shop where you can get magazines, gum, and stuff. We're not far from the school, only about two miles. You going to take the bus?"

"I guess so," I said. "I don't think Karl wants to drive me every day, especially since there is a bus."

"You call him Karl?" she asked quickly.

"Right now I do," I said, looking away.

"But Thelma you call Mom?"

"She wanted it that way from the start," I said. "You know what? You're right."

"What?"

"You *are* nosy."

She laughed. "Come on, I'll introduce you to Bernie Felder. I have a feeling you two will get along real well. Bernie's a genius, too."

"I'm not a genius," I corrected.

"Whatever." She sped up, and we walked to another ranch-style house with a brick facade. It looked like an expensive house. The landscaping was more elaborate than most, and the house was almost twice the size of Karl and Thelma's.

"What do Bernie's parents do?" I asked.

"His father owns a big tire store that services trucks," she said. "Bernie's an only child, like you."

"What about you?"

"I have a younger brother I ignore," she said. "My parents named him William, but they call him Buster."

"Buster?"

"When you see him, you'll see why. He looks like a Buster, and he's always busting things," she added. "Come on." She headed for the front door.

"Maybe we should call first," I said, but she pushed the door buzzer.

"I'd rather be unexpected," she said. "It's more fun."

A maid answered the door, and Helga asked for Bernie. A few moments later, a boy about my height with straggly red hair and light green eyes appeared. He wore a T-shirt that looked two sizes too big and a pair of jeans with sneakers and no socks. His face was pale with full red lips and a cleft chin.

"Hi, Bernie," Helga said.

He grimaced. "What do you want?" he demanded.

"That's not a very nice way to say hello," she remarked.

"I was in the middle of something," he said apologetically.

"You're not making bombs, are you? My mother always thinks Bernie's making bombs," she told me.

When she turned to me, Bernie finally looked my way, and his face filled with interest. "Who's this?"

"Our new neighbor, Bernie. If you hadn't

jumped down my throat, I would have been able to introduce you."

"I'm sorry," he said, turning to me. "Hello."

"Hello. I'm sorry we interrupted you, but . . ."

"It's all right." He looked embarrassed.

"Of course it's all right. What could Bernie be doing that can't be interrupted?" Helga asked.

"Whatever it is, it's important to him," I remarked dryly. She smirked, but Bernie's face softened.

"You just moved here?" he asked.

"If you didn't have your nose in a test tube all the time, you would have known about her," Helga said. "Her name is Crystal, and the Morrises adopted her."

"Oh?" he said, his lips forming a little circle as he gazed at me with even more interest.

"She was an orphan," Helga added. She stepped back to look at me. They both stared a moment, neither speaking.

"That's orphan, not alien," I said, and Bernie smiled.

"She reads a lot, and she's very smart," Helga continued. "Maybe even smarter than you, Bernie. That's why I thought you two should meet."

"Really?" he said, his interest in me growing even more.

"This was her idea. I'm sorry we bothered you." I started to turn away.

"Hey. That's okay," he called. "Come on in."

"Bernie's inviting us in," Helga said, raising her eyebrows. "You going to show us your laboratory, Bernie?"

"I don't have a laboratory," he snapped at her. She laughed. He turned to me. "Helga and her friends are always making stuff up about me."

"No, we don't, Bernie," she said. "Anyway, if we do, you should be honored we talk about you."

"Some honor," Bernie said. He stepped back, and Helga gestured emphatically for me to follow her into the house. I did.

Right away, I saw that Bernie's parents had a lot of money. There were paintings all over the walls, and the rooms were very big and full of expensive-looking furnishings. In the hallway to his room was a glass case filled with figurines. The floors were all covered with carpet so soft I felt as if I were walking on marshmallows.

Bernie's room was twice, maybe three times as big as mine. He had a large desk, a computer, and all sorts of hardware. I recognized a scanner and two printers. He even had his own fax machine. One wall was covered with charts that included the anatomy of the human body, a breakdown of the planets and some galaxies, an evolution time line, and a historical summary of American presidents and vice presidents with a listing of major events during their terms.

On the right were shelves that held a microscope, slides, scales, and even a Bunsen burner. I saw chemistry sets and shelves and shelves of reference books. What didn't he have? I wondered.

"You see?" Helga said. "He has a laboratory in his room."

"It's not a laboratory. I have a few things to develop my interests," he said defensively. "I want to get into genetic research someday."

"I don't even know what that means," Helga said.

He frowned and shook his head. "You know what this is?" he asked me, pointing to what looked like a Tinker Toy.

"Yes," I said. "It's a model of DNA."

"Right!" he said, his face becoming more animated than it had been since we met.

"What's DNA?" Helga asked.

"It has to do with genetics," Bernie said quickly. "You want to look at this? I put this together myself," he told me, and I drew closer.

"Don't you have a CD player or something in here?" Helga asked.

"No," he said quickly.

"Well, how do you listen to music?" she demanded.

"I listen on my computer when I want to listen to music," he said, and turned his back on her.

"This is like being back in school," she complained. "Not one movie poster, not one rock star poster, just all this . . . this educational stuff."

"It's very good," I said, nodding at his model. He beamed with pride.

"Come on, Crystal," Helga said. "I'll show you the rest of the neighborhood. Maybe Fern Peabody is home. She's going steady with Gary Lakewood, and she always has good stories to tell."

"I've got some interesting slides," Bernie said, ignoring her. "I just got them yesterday. They're from human embryos."

"Really?" I said.

"Ugh," Helga said. "Do they smell?"

"Of course not," Bernie snapped. "You should pay more attention in science class."

"Boring," she sang. "I'm going," she threatened.

Bernie held his hand on his microscope and looked at me.

"I'm staying," I said. I knew I should probably go with her to meet more of the neighborhood kids, but Bernie's projects really intrigued me.

"I knew it," Helga said. "Peas in a pod. I'll talk to you later," she threw back at me as she left Bernie's room.

He smiled. Then he brought his microscope to the desk and hurriedly set things up. "Sit right there," he said, pointing to his chair.

He slipped in the slides and began to talk about them as I gazed through the microscope. It really was like being at a class lecture, but I didn't mind. Some of it I knew, but most of it I didn't. He was so excited about having an audience, he went on and on and then brought out some other slides. I got so involved I didn't realize the time until I glanced at the clock by his bed.

"Oh, no," I said. "I'd better get home. I didn't tell my mother I was leaving. I didn't think I'd be away this long, and it's ten minutes past dinner."

"Right," he said with disappointment. He looked at the clock. "I don't eat dinner at any set time. I eat when I'm hungry."

"What about your parents?"

"They usually go out or eat at different times," he said.

"You never eat together?"

"Sometimes," he said as he put away his slides.

"Thanks for showing me everything," I told him as I walked to the door.

"Sure," he said.

He followed me out and down the hall.

"Maybe I'll see you again," I said, turning back to him just before leaving.

"Okay," he said. "Any time you want."

"Thank you," I said, and started away.

"Oh," he began.

I paused. "Yes?"

"I forgot. What's your name again?"

"It's Crystal," I said.

"I'm Bernie," he said.

I wanted to say, "I know, I remember your name. How could I not remember your name?" But he closed the door before I could add a word.

I hurried down the sidewalk. When I reached the house, I saw that my book was missing from the arm of the chair. It put a small panic in me because I realized Thelma had come looking for me. I quickened my steps and practically ran into the house.

"There," Karl said, hearing the door close and stepping out of the living room. "She's back, and she's all right."

I looked in and saw Thelma, her eyes bloodshot, her face pale. She was clutching her skirt and twisting the material anxiously.

"Oh, Crystal. I was sure something terrible had happened to you. When I walked out there to call you in for dinner and all I found was your book . . ."

"I'm sorry," I said both to Karl and to her. "A girl came by to introduce herself, and then we went for a walk and it took longer than I thought it would. We stopped to visit Bernie Felder and . . ."

"When I saw that book and the empty chair," Thelma continued, not listening to my explanation, "all I could think of was *Heart Shell* by Amanda Glass. That's the story about the little girl who was kidnapped and brought up by another family. There's a scene just like this. They find her children's book on the grass by her little chair. It's not until she's a young woman that she returns to her real parents."

I just stared.

"Well, she wasn't kidnapped," Karl said calmly, "so put all that horror out of your mind, Thelma."

He turned to me. "Next time, Crystal, please let us know where you are going," he chastised firmly.

"I'm sorry. I didn't think I'd be that long. I got too involved with Bernie Felder's slides. I never saw so much stuff in someone's house and . . ."

"It's all right. Dinner is a little late, but it's all right. Let's forget about it, Thelma, okay?" He looked at his watch. "There's no sense in wasting any more time over it."

"Right," she said, taking a deep breath. "It's all right." She smiled. "I'm just happy you're back," she said, as if I had been away for ages. "That's what the mother said in *Heart Shell*. I'm just happy you're back."

She hugged me as if she was afraid that if she ever let go, I'd disappear. I felt very confused. I was happy that someone cared so much about me, that someone could be sad and distraught just with the fear of my being gone, and yet I had to wonder. When Thelma looked at me, whom did she really see?

Me or the girl in *Heart Shell*?

4
Casting Call

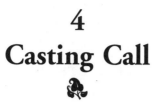

Thelma felt better at dinner after she started to tell me about her soap opera. Because I was still feeling guilty for what I had done, I pretended to be interested in the story and the characters. However, it seemed silly to me that people fell in and out of such passionate love affairs so easily, that people betrayed each other despite how long they had known and trusted each other, and that children could despise their parents so much. For Thelma, however, what happened on the soaps was gospel. It was as if some biblical prophet wrote the scripts.

To some extent, I couldn't blame her. Most of the leading men seemed godlike, perfect. The women were glamorous even when they woke in the morning. When I innocently asked if we were to believe they went to sleep wearing makeup, Thelma said when someone is that beautiful, she always looks as if she's wearing makeup.

"I never met anyone that beautiful," I remarked, and she laughed in such a way it

made me feel as though I were the unin-
formed one.

"That's why they're my special people,"
she said. "See why I like to watch my soaps?"

I suppose it was all right to watch them, I
thought, as long as we remembered that life
wasn't really like a soap opera. Our lives
weren't filled with dramatic events, and people rarely felt as passionate about anything
as they constantly did on that small screen.

"What happened between Nevada and
Johnny Lee touched my heart," she exclaimed toward the end of dinner. She
smiled, and tears filled the deep furrows
around her eyes. Then she looked at Karl
and reached for his hand.

Karl glanced at me when she put her hand
over his. He looked uncomfortable, but he
didn't stop her or pull away, and I wondered
what sort of love life my new parents shared.
In all of the pictures of them that were in the
house, they looked so formal, Karl always
standing stiffly, Thelma always looking as if
she was afraid she would make a terrible social mistake.

Later in the evening, I discovered just
what sort of a romantic life they had. I had
gone up to bed before them as usual. When I
left them in the living room, Karl was reading *Business Weekly* and Thelma was watch-

ing a videotape she had made of a recent soap she had to miss so she could keep a dentist appointment. I finished reading my book and felt a little tired. Once again, I apologized to Thelma for giving her a scare earlier, and I promised I would never do anything like that again.

"You're so sweet to say that, dear. Karl and I knew from the moment we set eyes on you that you were a responsible young lady and things like this wouldn't happen often, if at all. All is forgiven," she said with an unexpected, theatrical air, her voice rising, her arms sweeping the air in an over-the-top dramatic gesture. Even Karl lowered his magazine and gazed at her with concern for a moment.

She held her arms out for me, and I went to her so she could embrace me, rocking back and forth as she spoke in a chantlike voice. "We must be good to each other, kind and considerate and loving. You have suffered so much, my little darling, and my life has been so empty without you. The love we all have for each other is almost holy. Always, forever and ever, always fit us into the corners of your life. Do you promise, Crystal? Do you?"

"Yes," I said, not sure what it was I was promising to do.

She sighed deeply but still held on to me.

"Thelma," Karl said gently, "the child is tired and wants to go to bed."

"Yes, to bed," she said. "Good night, dear. Good night, good night, good night," she sang in my ear, and kissed me on the top of my head.

"Good night," I told them, and went upstairs.

Could it be, I wondered, that someone really did need me more than I needed her? No one had ever held me like that, much less held me that long, and although female staff members at the orphanages had kissed me occasionally, those kisses were quick smacks of their lips, almost like little pats on my cheeks and forehead. I felt nothing, no love, no deep concern. No, I thought, despite all her faults, Thelma did make me feel wanted, and what was more important than that?

I had just closed my eyes and tucked the blanket under my chin when I heard soft footsteps in the hallway. Then, in a voice I almost didn't recognize, I heard Thelma calling. It was confusing. I had to sit up to listen harder.

"Johnny Lee," I heard. "Please, please forgive me. Please, don't hate me."

At first, I thought she was simply repeating lines she loved from the show she had seen, but then I heard Karl say, "I don't hate you. I could never hate you, Nevada."

"I want to give myself to you," she said. "I want to give myself to you like I have never given myself to anyone, Johnny Lee."

"I know. I want you, too," Karl said.

There was a silence and then the soft sound of footsteps. I went to the door and opened it a crack to peek out. There they were in the hallway, kissing fully on the lips. I was mesmerized. Karl put his left hand under Thelma's blouse.

"No," she said, pulling back.

"Why not?" he asked, raising his voice.

"It doesn't happen like that. Nothing like that happens until she cries," Thelma said.

He pulled his hand out from under her blouse and held her hips.

"Okay, okay," he said. "I forgot."

"You're ruining it," she accused.

"I said I forgot."

"Start over," she commanded.

"What? Why?"

"You've got to start over," she insisted.

"That's silly, Thelma."

"Don't call me Thelma!" she exclaimed. "You're ruining it!"

"All right, all right. I'm sorry. I'll start over."

He turned from her, and I closed the door softly so neither of them would see me spying. My heart was pounding so hard, however, I was afraid they would hear the thumping in my chest. I listened.

Karl went down the hallway and closed a door. Then he opened it.

"Nevada," he called.

I opened my door again. Thelma was standing with her back to me now. She turned slowly, her face so different. She really looked as if she was on some sort of stage.

"Johnny Lee," she said, and wiped her cheeks. I could see she was crying real tears. "Please, please forgive me. Please, don't hate me."

"I don't hate you. I could never hate you, Nevada."

"I want to give myself to you," she repeated. "I want to give myself to you like I have never given myself to anyone, Johnny Lee."

"I know. I want you, too," Karl repeated his lines just as he'd said them before.

He stepped up to her, and they embraced but did not kiss. This time, he kept his hands on her hips. She started to cry, her whole body shaking. He embraced her and held her against his chest, kissing her hair, her cheeks, and then holding her head up softly so he could kiss her lips.

Then his hand returned to the bottom of

her blouse and moved up over her breast again. She moaned.

"Will it be different tonight, Johnny Lee? Will it be going to the moon and back?"

"Just like I promised," Karl said. He lowered his right arm around her waist, and they turned toward their bedroom. Thelma laid her head on his shoulder as they walked toward their room. I watched until they disappeared inside, the door closing softly behind them.

I didn't want to eavesdrop on them, but curiosity was like a magnet drawing me toward the wall between our two bedrooms. I put the tips of my fingers against it. Their voices were muffled, as were Thelma's sobs. I brought my ear to the wall and closed my eyes.

"Oh, Johnny Lee," she said. "Touch me everywhere this time. Do what you promised you would do. Make my body sing."

"I will."

They were quiet, but I heard the distinct sound of the bedsprings. Her moans grew louder, longer. There was a combination of moans and cries that made me even more curious. Was lovemaking painful as well as pleasureful? Why wasn't he crying out, too?

Finally, after a long, loud cry, everything grew silent. I listened for a while longer and then retreated to my own bed. Was that the way it was supposed to be? I knew every scientific detail. I could describe the hormones, the movement of blood, even the nerve impulses, but the emotions were so confusing. Sex was one thing, but sex with love was supposed to be another.

Suddenly, I heard a door open and some more whispering. I got out of bed and went to my own door again.

"Good night, good night, parting is such sweet sorrow . . ."

They both laughed.

Karl was in the hallway looking back at their bedroom. He blew a kiss. He was fully dressed.

"I wish you could stay," Thelma said.

"So do I."

"Someday."

"Someday," he said, and turned. I stepped back as he walked past my bedroom. I heard Thelma close her door.

I wish you could stay? Where was he going? What did this mean?

For a long moment, it was very quiet. Then Karl's footsteps echoed down the hallway as if he was deliberately trying to be loud. I opened the door again and watched him walk past to their bedroom. When he opened the door, I heard him say,

"You still up, Thelma?"

"I couldn't sleep," she replied, "so I decided to read a little, but I'm tired now."

"Good. It's bedtime," he said, and entered the bedroom, closing the door.

I put my ear to the wall and listened. I heard water running in their bathroom sink and a toilet flush. Neither of them spoke for the longest time, and then I heard Karl say, "Good night, Thelma."

"Good night, Karl."

All was quiet. I returned to my bed, but I didn't fall asleep for quite a while. How could adults be like children, playing games and pretending? What would love be like for me if it ever happened to me? What sort of a man would find me attractive, or would no man find me attractive and I would be forced to imagine a life, too?

How I wished I had a big sister or a close friend, someone in whom I would be unafraid to confide, someone I could trust with my deepest hidden secrets. That was what was truly wonderful about family, I thought. When you had one, you didn't have to keep all of your troubled feelings and fears simmering under a pot. You could go to them and be unafraid to lift the lid. You could help each other and keep each other from being afraid.

Wasn't that the most important thing?

Of course, the next morning, I said nothing about what I had seen and heard Thelma and Karl do the night before. I felt guilty for spying on them anyway. Karl had made plans to return home from work early so he, Thelma, and I could go shopping for things I would need at the start of school the next day. At first, he was just going to tell Thelma where the best places were and have us go ourselves, but she complained that this was a family thing and he should be a part of it. He thought about it and agreed.

"You have to forgive me," he told me. "I'm not used to thinking like a parent. Of course I'll be here. Of course I want to be part of everything important."

I know he tried to relax and make it seem like fun, but it just wasn't in his nature to treat purchasing as anything less than a serious project. Thelma had made a list of clothing, and I had made a list of school supplies. Karl took our lists and researched everything. He knew exactly where the best prices were for every item. Colors, fashions, and styles played the least role. Our shopping was planned efficiently, down to where we would eat dinner and even what was the best food value.

"A family," Karl explained as we ate, "is really a small enterprise, a business venture, a partnership. The more that's planned, the better it will be."

"Karl even planned our wedding and honeymoon so as to take advantage of some good specials, didn't you, Karl?" Thelma said proudly.

"Yes. It was off-season, after Labor Day, the best time to find good values."

"But was it someplace you wanted to go?" I asked.

"If it's a good value for the dollar, it's where I want to be," Karl replied. "People pay more for the things they want and need because they don't do the necessary research and planning."

"Karl has even bought our final resting places and has our funerals arranged, don't you, Karl?" Thelma said. "He did it shortly after we got married."

"That soon?" I asked innocently.

"Having family members make final arrangements is one of the biggest rip-offs. You need to make your arrangements when you're alive. Don't be afraid to think ahead, Crystal. Never let anyone intimidate you into thinking you're being too practical. You can never be too practical," he instructed.

Thelma's parents had asked us to stop

over at their house when we were finished shopping for my school things. They said they had something they wanted to give me. As we drove there, Karl reminded Thelma of the time and how long he wanted us to stay.

My new grandparents had a small but cozy ranch-style home. Thelma said that Karl had found it for them shortly after her father retired.

"It fit their new budget perfectly," he said with pride. "That's another thing you can't think about too soon: your retirement. Most people don't put away enough and suffer because of it."

"But not us," Thelma chimed.

"No, not us," Karl agreed with a smile.

What my grandparents had for me was a brown leather briefcase with my name embroidered in gold letters on the outside. I was more pleased with it than anything else I had gotten that day.

"It wasn't necessary to buy real leather, Martha," Karl told my grandmother.

"Of course it was," she replied, and smiled at me. "Why shouldn't she have the nicest things?"

We had tea, and Grandma served her homemade sugar cookies, which I thought were delicious. Then she told stories about her days at school. She had attended a smaller, rural school. She talked about how she had to walk almost a mile and a half to get there.

"Even in the snow!"

"Even in the snow because we didn't have schoolbuses like you do now."

Grandpa tried to match her stories with his own, and she kept correcting him and saying he was exaggerating. They were both funny and delightful. I was really beginning to enjoy myself when Karl announced it was time to go home.

"Tomorrow's her first day at a new school," he declared when my grandmother complained we hadn't even been there an hour. "She needs an early night."

"Well, you call me as soon as you can afterward and tell me all about your first day, Crystal," Grandma said.

"I will. Thank you again for the briefcase," I said.

She hugged me. "Our pleasure. We don't have much to spend our money on these days but medicines and such."

"You've got the best health plan," Karl said.

"Oh, I don't want to talk about that," Grandma said quickly. "Now that we have a granddaughter, I don't want to talk about my ailments."

We said good night and left.

"If they didn't have the plan I got them," Karl muttered when we got into the car, "she would be bankrupt paying for that heart medicine. Those prescriptions are very expensive."

"She knows," Thelma said. "She's just excited about Crystal. As we all are," she added. "I wish I could attend class with you tomorrow, Crystal. I wish I was starting over again."

"It's not easy to change schools," Karl said. "It's nothing to envy."

"I know. Did you ever read *Love on Wheels*, about that family that lives in a motor home and has to go from place to place, town to town, following farm work?"

"No," I replied.

"Just when Stacy finds the love of her life, she has to leave him. I'll give it to you," Thelma promised. "In fact, you should read all my books. Then we could talk about them, about all my special people. Wouldn't that be nice?"

I didn't answer fast enough.

"She'll have too much to do now that school's starting," Karl said, coming to my rescue.

"She has to have time off, doesn't she? What's a better way to spend it than reading?" Thelma countered.

How funny, I thought. I would get assignments at school and assignments at home. There was no doubt in my mind which ones my mother thought were more important.

Once I got home and put all my new things away, I realized Karl wasn't so wrong. I did need to get to bed. I was so nervous about the next day and what it would bring, sleep was as hard to grasp and hold as an icicle. He was right about another thing, too. It wasn't easy to change schools, to make new friends, to get used to different teachers and rules.

It was almost like losing your memory and starting over as a different person.

And wasn't that exactly what I was, a new person with a new last name and a new family?

My old self curled up in some dark corner, shivering, naked, and alone.

"What will become of me?" she asked.

"In time," I told her, "you will disappear."

It was a cruel thought, but it was what I hoped would happen, wasn't it?

It was also what made me cower in my own new corner of the world, just as naked and just as frightened about tomorrow.

5

A New Friend

To my surprise, Karl decided he would take me to school every morning, but I had to come home on the bus. It wasn't a problem, because the route was just a few minutes out of his way to work. Nevertheless, it was really Thelma who had suggested it.

"It will give you two more time to get to know each other," she said. I was waiting for her to add the name of a book and the names of characters in a similar situation, but she didn't. Karl considered and decided she was right.

Karl and I hadn't spent all that much time together without Thelma. She was always the one who began conversations or asked questions. When Karl and I drove off that first morning, I remembered he didn't like being distracted from his driving, so I didn't say anything. For a while, we drove in complete silence, interrupted occasionally by his describing the route we were taking.

"What is your favorite subject?" he finally asked.

"Science, especially biology," I replied. He nodded, his eyes fixed firmly on the car ahead of us.

"I enjoyed science, but math was always my favorite. I never told anyone," he said, flashing a small smile at me before whipping his head back to watch the road, "but to me numbers are living things. They resemble one-, two-, and multicelled animals, depending on the combinations, formulas, and so on."

"That's interesting," I said. He liked that, and I was glad. Talking to him had taken the edge off my nervousness. I was distracted enough not to worry about my imminent entrance to a new school full of strangers.

"I feel like I'm creating something when I work out my accounts and balance sheets. Everything has a way of relating to everything else. I bet you can understand what I'm saying," he added.

"I think so," I said, even though I wasn't sure I did, and he gave me a wider smile.

"When we were trying to make a baby, I was hoping he or she would grow up to be someone I could talk to, someone who was bright enough to understand. That's why I was so happy when Thelma said she liked you, too. Most kids have fluff in their heads today," he continued, his eyes darkening.

"They don't get serious about life until it's almost too late or, in many cases, too late. There are too many distractions. Don't tell Thelma I said this, but I think it's good that you don't want to spend all your free time staring into a light bulb."

"A light bulb?"

"That's all television is to me, a light bulb with idiotic stuff on its surface," he muttered. "I don't even like the way they report the news. The news is a comic book these days."

I was surprised at how forcefully he condemned television. I could see him rushing into people's homes and smashing screens with a sledge hammer, yet when it came to his own home, he sat silently reading his magazines while Thelma sat entranced.

"Thelma really loves her programs," I said.

"I know. And I appreciate how you humor her," he added with a smile.

"Did she always spend so much time watching them?"

He was quiet, concentrating on his driving. We stopped at a traffic light, and he took a deep breath. "She didn't tell you everything about our attempt to have a baby of our own," he confessed. "We tried in vitro fertilization. You know what that is?"

"Yes," I said. "Taking out a woman's egg,

inserting sperm into it in a Petri dish, and placing it back in the woman's womb."

"You are smart. Yes. Well, it didn't work for her. She miscarried. She was very depressed afterward. Very depressed," he emphasized, raising his eyebrows and widening his eyes. "It was then that she began to watch television. Getting involved in the stories was the only thing that excited her. I couldn't oppose it." He paused and then glanced at me quickly. "I didn't want to tell you this so soon," he continued, "but you're my big hope."

"Me? How?"

"I'm hoping she'll become so involved with you and real-life things that she'll start to drift away from the make-believe world. I was holding my breath when you first came to our home, waiting to see if you were going to get sucked into those soap operas with her. You don't know how glad I am that you haven't been," he said.

"I like a good story," I confessed.

"Sure, who doesn't? But it can't become your whole life. It does for people who have nothing but popcorn in their heads. You're not one of them. You're a serious young lady. You're going to be someone, and I want to be there when they hand you your first diploma."

I smiled. He sounded proud already, and I hadn't done a thing. In fact, it was the first time I felt he sounded like a real father.

"I hope you're there too," I told him.

He seemed to relax in his seat and soften his grip around the steering wheel. We really were getting to know each other better. Thelma had made a good suggestion.

"I'll tell you another one of my secrets," he offered. "I even view people in terms of numbers."

"How do you do that?" I asked.

"Easy." He paused as if he wasn't going to say any more, but he had a small smile on his lips again. "Some people are positive numbers, and many are negative. Didn't you ever hear someone say, 'He's a complete zero'? Well, that's how I group people in my mind, only I have categories in the negatives, too." He laughed. "My immediate superior is a minus ten. He used to be a minus five, but he's gotten worse."

"I've heard about women being rated like that," I said. "A beautiful woman is supposed to be a ten."

"Yeah, but that's a stupid use of numbers," he said angrily. It was as if numbers were his province and no one else had a right to use them. "You don't measure someone solely on the way he or she looks. It's what's going on in here," he said, stabbing his temple with his forefinger so hard I imagined the pain, "that counts. Counts, get it?" he said, smiling.

I nodded.

"There she blows," he cried, nodding ahead of us. I saw the school building down the street. Arriving buses were emptying their passengers. Old friends were hugging and talking excitedly to one another. They all had that first-day-of-school look, the clean and crisp appearance their parents most likely imposed on them.

"You know the number of the bus that takes you home?" Karl asked.

"Yes."

"Okay, have a great first day," he said, pulling to the curb. He looked at me as if he wanted to give me a kiss good-bye. I waited a moment expecting it, but he just smiled and nodded again, squirming in his seat as if he was uncomfortable. We were still orbiting each other like strangers, waiting for something that would make us truly father and daughter. Why was it so much harder for me than it was for all those young people laughing and shouting in front of the school? What wonderful things had they done to deserve their families, their mommies and daddies? What terrible thing had I done to be born alone?

" 'Bye," I cried, and hopped out of the car. I turned to wave, but he was pulling away, his attention locked on the driveway in front of him.

First days of school always had a special feeling to them. The desks, the blackboards, the hallways, the bathrooms, windows, and floors were squeaky clean. You could still smell the detergents, wood polish, glass cleaner, and fresh paint. Voices, footsteps, and bells all had a deeper, longer echo. There was an electricity of expectation and anticipation in the air, as well as some mystery. What was going to be required of us? How well would we get along with our new teachers? How well would we get along with one another? Those who had been here before studied one another to discover the changes a summer of fun or work or both had effected on their bodies, their faces, and, most of all, their personalities.

Girls and boys alike were exploring new styles, wore their hair differently, dressed more maturely. Those who were more insecure about themselves held themselves back toward the rear, in the shadows, out of the direct flow of conversations and attention, while the confident strutted with their heads high, seeking to reclaim their turf quickly and eyeing every possible contender with suspicion.

New kids were interesting and yet threatening. I could almost hear their suspicion when they looked at me. The girl who was expected to win the lead in the school play wondered if I would try out and take her part away. The students who were at the top of their classes, racing toward the awards and honors, wondered if I would be real competition. Girls who were leaders of their little cliques feared I might be more sophisticated and win away their loyal followers. Girls and even boys who fell outside the circle of social life hoped I might be another one of them, a friend, a buoy to cling to in the sea of turmoil adults called the teenage years, adolescence.

I was here. I had landed, and I was living with a family now. No one could fix the label of orphan on my forehead like the mark of Cain and make me feel so different that I saw curiosity and rejection in the eyes of those who were supposed to be friends. At least, that was what I hoped.

The moment I spotted Helga talking and laughing with a group of girls near the girls' room, I felt a dark foreboding take hold of my heart. She saw me and nudged someone, and they all grew quiet and looked my way.

"Hi," she called, waving me toward her.

"Hi."

"You didn't take the bus this morning, so I didn't know whether or not you were still living with Karl and Thelma," she said.

"Why wouldn't I be?" I shot back.

She looked at her friends and then at me and shrugged.

"I just wondered," she said, shifting her weight from one leg to the other and smiling again. "I introduced Crystal to Bernie Felder. We went over to his house, and she didn't want to leave. How long did you stay?"

"A while," I said. So that was it, I thought. I was being punished for not doing exactly what she had wanted, for defying her and staying with Bernie.

"Crystal's a genius, too," she said with an ugly twist in her lips.

"I'm far from a genius, but I am polite," I said. I turned to the others. "My name is Crystal Morris."

They stared a moment, and then a short brunette with a face like a little doll, her features small and perfect, stuck out her hand.

"I'm Alicia."

"I'm Mona," said another girl, with a rounder face, straight light brown hair, and brown eyes. Her fingers were short and stubby.

"My name is Rachael Peterson," a girl almost as tall as Helga said in a very formal voice. She didn't offer her hand, but she looked at my briefcase. "Is that real leather?" she asked.

"Yes."

"Very nice," she said.

"Thank you. My grandparents gave it to me."

"Grandparents? How can you have grandparents?" Helga asked quickly.

"Thelma's parents are my grandparents," I said dryly. "That's how it works."

"So how did you get to school this morning?" Helga asked, ignoring my sarcasm. "You didn't come with Bernie, did you?"

"Karl took me on the way to work. He's going to take me every morning, but I'll go home on the bus," I explained.

"Still calling him Karl, I see," Helga said, shifting her eyes to her friends. She smiled wryly, her lips twisting again.

"Well, I wasn't as lucky as the rest of you. I wasn't born into a family," I said. I saw Alicia's eyebrows lift. Mona's eyes filled with confusion.

"I told you she was very intelligent," Helga said quickly.

Alicia and Mona nodded, but Rachael continued just to stare down at me.

"It doesn't take a lot of intelligence to know not to say things that will embarrass someone who is new and a stranger to the school," I said. "That usually shows a lack of it." I turned and walked toward my homeroom just as the bell rang.

Bernie Felder was in my homeroom. He nodded when he saw me, his eyes softening as if they saw my distress at being new and unsure of myself, but he didn't sit near me. He took the last seat in the first row, as if that seat had been waiting for him all summer. Our homeroom teacher didn't seem to care where anyone sat, so I sat up front and opened my briefcase.

Homeroom was extended on the first day so all the school's rules could be explained. Most of the students paid little attention. Even our homeroom teacher seemed bored with it and looked relieved when the bell for passing to the first class rang.

I did make some friends during the course of the school day: a pair of redheaded twins named Rea and Zoe, who told me their parents deliberately had looked for names with the same number of letters, a heavy black girl named Haley Thomas, and a tall, very thin boy named Randal Wolfe who was the school's chess champion. There was another girl named Ashley who remained in the background, too shy to say anything. The twins wore matching dresses and had their hair styled in a similar fashion. They told me they enjoyed playing tricks on people and even their teachers by pretending to be each other from time to time.

"When we get married, we'll do it to our husbands, too," Rea said, laughing.

We all sat at the same table and ate lunch together. I looked for Bernie, but he wasn't in the cafeteria. Later, when I saw him in the hallway, I asked him where he had been. He looked embarrassed and very nervous because I had stopped him to talk. His eyes shifted from side to side, and then he looked down at the floor when he replied.

"I eat lunch in the bio lab. Mr. Friedman lets me. I get work done and sometimes help him set up his equipment for his classes. He lets me run some of my own experiments from time to time, usually after school," he added, and looked up. "How do you like your first day so far?"

"It's okay. I really like my English teacher and our math teacher," I said. Bernie was in my math class.

He nodded.

"Mr. Albert is the best one to have for geometry. We're lucky. I gotta go to gym," he said, moving away. "I'm always late for gym."

I watched him walk quickly down the hallway, and then I went to the library for my study period. I didn't see him again until the end of the school day when I stepped onto the bus. Helga was up front with Alicia. She smiled at me.

"Bernie's in the back," she said.

"You're not funny," I told her, but she laughed anyway.

I made my way back, passing Ashley, who sat alone looking as if she wanted to ask me to sit with her. Bernie glanced up at me and then looked at the textbook he had opened. I sat across from him and gazed out the window.

"Your friend Helga's been saying things about us," I heard him say, and turned.

"What did you say?"

"Some of the guys in my gym class were saying things about us," he told me.

"First, she's not my friend. I met her for the first time when I met you. And second, I don't think I could be friends with her. She's not very nice."

He didn't move his lips, but his eyes smiled.

"I wondered how you could be friends

with her," he said, and then looked at his book again.

We rode in silence all the way back to our neighborhood. My stop was before his. I said good-bye, and he nodded and looked at his book again. Helga had already gotten off. She was waiting for me on the sidewalk.

"I'm not trying to be mean," she said. "I was just teasing you. I'd really like to be friends."

"Why?" I asked her.

"Why?"

"Yes, why do you want to be friends with me?"

"I don't know. Why does anyone become friends with anyone?" she replied.

"Usually because they have something in common, they like the same things, they want to do the same things," I said.

"So?"

"So when you think of something you and I might like to do together, let me know," I said, and walked away. Maybe I was being unforgiving; maybe I just didn't trust her. Whatever the reason, it felt good.

I heard the television set when I entered the house and knew what soap Thelma was watching and how important it was to her, but I remembered what Karl had said to me in the morning and how much he was hoping I would help bring Thelma back to reality.

"Hi," I said, and she looked up.

"Oh, Crystal, you're back from school. I want to hear all about your first day. Just a minute, and there will be a commercial," she said.

"I'll go change first," I said.

She nodded, her eyes already drawn back to the screen. When I returned, the television was turned off and Thelma was sitting quietly in the rocking chair, moving back and forth slightly and staring down at the floor.

"Mom?" I said, and she looked up, her eyes blank for a moment and then suddenly coming on like a pair of tiny lamps.

"Oh, Crystal. I'm stunned. Just at the end, Brock told his mother he's gay, and all this time I thought he was in love with Megan. I mean, I never would have known." She shook her head. "What's her mother going to say?"

"Um, I'm not sure," I said, not knowing how to answer her. I decided instead to tell her about my day. "I like my new school."

"What? Oh, yes, the school. How was your first day?"

"It was good. I like most of my teachers."

"Did you make any friends?" she asked, as

if that was the main reason for school.

"A few," I said. "I ate lunch with a pair of twins."

"A pair of twins? Isn't that something? Girls?"

"Yes, Rea and Zoe. They're very nice."

"Rea? Where did I hear that name before? Rea? Oh, yes, *Yesterday's Children*. Rea was Lindsey's lost sister."

"This Rea is real, Mom. I can call her on the phone and speak with her. I can go places with her. I can study with her. I can touch her. She's real."

Thelma stared at me as if I had lost my mind. "That's nice, dear. Oh, I better get started on dinner. Would you like to set the table?"

"Of course," I said, feeling frustrated.

When Karl came home, he asked me many more questions about school. In fact, we had one of the longest conversations we had had since I arrived. Every once in a while, both of us would look at Thelma. She would simply smile.

"It's so nice to have real family conversations around the dinner table," she finally said.

Karl beamed and then winked at me. I felt as if he and I were co-conspirators.

Right after dinner, the phone rang and

Karl called to me. "It's for you," he said.

"Oh, good," Thelma said. "She's making friends quickly."

I couldn't imagine who it could be. I hoped it wasn't Helga.

"Hello," I said hesitantly.

"I got my new slides today, cross sections of human heart tissue. I thought you might be interested," Bernie said without saying hello.

"Yes, I would be interested," I replied.

"Can you come over?"

"Now?"

He didn't answer.

"I suppose so," I said. I held my hand over the mouthpiece and asked Karl and Thelma, telling them what Bernie had to show me.

"As long as you don't stay out too late," Karl said. Thelma just smiled.

"I'll be there as soon as I finish helping clean up our dinner dishes," I told Bernie. He hung up without saying good-bye.

"You don't have to help me," Thelma said. "It's not much. Go on."

"Are you sure, Mom?"

"Of course."

I went to my room and got my light jacket. When I started out, Thelma was at the door.

"You're going to go look at cross sections of a human heart?" she asked.

"That's what he says."

She shook her head. "I'm sure that's interesting. Is he a good-looking boy?"

"He's all right," I said. "I'm really more interested in the slides."

She tilted her head like a puppy when it hears a totally confusing noise. Then she smiled, laughed, and said, "Wouldn't it be something if you could see love under a microscope, too? Then we'd know if someone was really heartsick." She laughed again. "Have a good time," she called back as she returned to the kitchen.

I shook my head and laughed myself. It would be something if we could see feelings and know if they were honest and true.

Then everyone would know if I really was more interested in the slides.

6
My Tutor

Bernie answered the door himself. The house was dark and quiet.

"Maid's night off," he muttered, and stepped back.

"Where are your parents?" I asked as I entered. After having lived all my life in orphanages and now living with Thelma, who kept the television on the way some people kept on lights, it seemed strange to enter a home that was so silent.

"Out," he said. "At a meeting or a dinner or something. They left numbers in the kitchen, but I didn't look at them. Come on," he said, leading the way down the hall to his room.

He had the microscope out and the new slides beside it. Next to that was a plastic replica of the human heart.

"These cells come from heart muscle," he said, and glanced into the microscope. He had yet to look at me directly.

I stepped up beside him and waited, and then he moved to the side.

"Go on, take a look," he said.

I sat and looked through the eyepiece. I had to adjust the focus to fit my vision, but it soon came in clear, and I was amazed at the detail I could see.

"This came with it," he explained, and read from a sheet of printed material.

" 'We studied cardiac explants and autopsy hearts of patients with chronic congestive heart failure caused by either a dilated cardiomyopathy or ischemic heart disease and compared them with normal hearts. In control hearts, endothelial cells rarely were positive for PAL-E. In hearts of patients with ischemic cardiomyopathies, there was distinct staining with this marker.

" 'Conclusions: A phenotypic shift in endothelial antigen expression of the coronary microvasculature occurs in both ischemic hearts and hearts with dilated cardiomyopathies, as revealed by PAL-E, compared with control hearts. The change may relate to compensatory mechanisms in long-standing chronic heart failure.' "

He put the paper down as if he assumed I understood any or all of it. I shook my head. "Where did you get all this?"

"A friend of my father's works at a cardiovascular research lab in Minnesota. He sent it. My father tells everyone I'm some sort of scientific genius, and they send me things." He gazed at the sheet. "This is heavy research."

"Let me see it," I said, and he handed me the paper. I reread most of what he had read aloud. "No way could I understand it." I shook my head. "This might as well be in a foreign language. I mean, I know what some of the words mean, but putting it all together . . . I guess they've found a way to diagnose a heart problem."

"Right," he said. He looked relieved that I didn't know much more than he did.

I gazed at the cell under the microscope again.

"It is interesting to know that this was once part of a human being," I said.

"I didn't show you half of it before. I've got cells from all sorts of human organs," he said with more excitement in his voice. He went to his special small file cabinet and opened a drawer. Gazing in, he read from the labels. "Liver, kidney, lungs, ovaries, the prostate, even some brain cells."

It was almost as if I had gone shopping at a department store for human cells and he was the salesman. I couldn't help but smile.

"What's so funny?" he asked sharply.

"Nothing," I said, not wanting to make him feel bad. "It's just unusual to see someone have all that in his room."

He slammed the drawer closed. "I thought you would be interested and even excited about it," he said.

"I am! Really, Bernie, I am," I cried.

He looked at me sideways, his eyes narrow with suspicion.

"I mean it. I'm sorry," I said.

He hesitated and then opened the drawer again. "You want to see anything else?" he asked.

"I'd like to see a brain cell."

He brought it over and set it up in the microscope. Then he stepped back, and I looked.

"You know there are about ten billion of those in your brain," he said as I studied the cell. "The brain controls every vital function of our bodies and even controls our emotions like hate, anger, love."

This time, I did laugh.

"What?"

"My mother, Thelma," I said, looking up at him, "asked if we could see love in the heart cell."

"That's an old medieval belief that love is centered in the heart. I told you. It's all in the brain," he corrected. "And you can't see feelings."

"I know. It was just a silly little idea."

"Right. It is silly," he said. He started to put away the slides. "Do you know what you want to be?" he asked me.

"Maybe a doctor. I like writing, too. I might even be a teacher," I said, and he grimaced. "You wouldn't want to be a teacher?" I asked.

"Hardly," he said, turning back to me. "I couldn't put up with giggly girls and jocks and all their problems."

"But good teachers are important," I said.

"I'm not going to do that," he insisted. "Pure research is what I want to do. I don't want to put up with stupid people."

"But why do it if you don't care about people?" I asked.

"I care. I just don't want to be . . . interrupted and annoyed."

"Not everyone will be annoying," I insisted.

He stared at me. "You like to argue, don't you?"

"No, but I don't mind having a discussion," I said. He finally smiled, a small twitch of his lips in the corners and a brighter light in his green eyes.

"You hungry?"

"No. I just finished supper, remember? Didn't you eat your supper?"

"No. I got too involved with my new slides

and forgot. The maid left me something to warm up. You want to watch me eat?" he asked.

"Is it as much fun as looking at the slides?"

He laughed. "You're the first girl I've met who's easy to talk to," he said.

"Thanks, I guess."

"Come on," he said, and I followed him to the kitchen. It was three times the size of ours and had appliances that looked as if they belonged in a space station.

"What is that?" I asked, pointing at a machine on the counter.

"That? A cappuccino machine. My mother likes her cappuccino after dinner. Whenever she eats at home," he added. He opened the giant refrigerator and took out a covered plate. "Lasagna," he said. "I just have to put it in the microwave for a couple of minutes."

I watched him do so.

"How about something to drink? Lemonade, iced tea, soda, milk, beer?"

"Beer!"

"You never had it?" he asked skeptically.

"Not really," I said. "I'll have whatever you have."

He poured us both some iced tea. There was a place setting all ready for him at the dining-room table. It was a large, oval, dark oak table with thick legs. There were twelve captain's chairs set around the table, and above us a large chandelier dangled on a gold chain. Behind us, the wall was all mirror. Against the far wall was a grand hutch with matching wood, filled with dishes and glasses that all looked very expensive.

Bernie brought his food out and set it down. "Our maid is a good cook. Otherwise I'd starve," he quipped.

"Your mother doesn't cook?"

"My mother? She couldn't boil water without burning it," he said.

"You can't burn water."

"It's a joke. At least, it was supposed to be."

"How often do you eat alone like this?" I asked.

He paused and thought, as if I had given him a difficult question to answer. "On the average, I'd say four times a week."

"Four!"

"I said average, so you know that there are weeks when it's more," he lectured.

"You should be a teacher," I said. "You like pointing things out, and I bet you love correcting people."

He gazed at me a moment and then smiled. "You want to do our math homework after I eat?" he asked.

"I did it before dinner," I said.

"I did it on the bus," he countered.

"So why did you ask?"

He shrugged. "I thought I'd help you."

"Maybe I would have helped you."

He laughed again and then grew serious, his eyes small and fixed on me intently. Bernie had a way of looking at people as if they were under his microscope. It made me a little uncomfortable.

"What?" I said.

"I was wondering what it was like for you, living in an orphanage," he said.

"Here I go again." I moaned.

"What?"

"That's all anyone wants to know."

"I was just curious, from a scientific point of view," he added.

"You really want to know? I'll tell you, it was hard," I fired at him. "I didn't feel like I was anyone. I felt like I was dangling, waiting for my life to start. Everyone is jealous of whatever lucky thing happens to anyone else. Counselors, social workers, adults who come around to choose a child make you feel like you're . . ."

"Under a microscope?"

"Yes, exactly. And it's no fun. You're afraid to make friends with someone because he or she might be gone the next month."

103

"What about your real parents?" he asked.

"What about them?"

"Why did they give you up?"

"My mother had me out of wedlock," I said. "She was too sick to take care of me. I don't know who my father is, and I don't care."

"Why not?"

"I just don't," I said, tears burning under my eyelids. "So, to answer your question, it wasn't pleasant," I concluded in a tone that was much sharper than I intended.

Bernie didn't wince or look away. He just nodded. "I understand," he said.

"Really? I don't see how you could unless you were an orphan, too," I replied, not in a very generous mood.

He looked around the room and then at me. "I *am* an orphan," he said nonchalantly, as if it was an obvious fact. "An orphan with parents. It's always been like this. My mother treats me as if I was some sort of space creature. She had a difficult pregnancy with me, and she had to have a cesarean delivery. You know what that is, right?"

"Of course."

"So she never had any more children, and if she could have, she probably would have aborted me. Once, when she was angry at me for something, she said that," he added hotly.

"How terrible," I said, shaking my head.

"My father is disappointed that I'm not a jock. He tries to get me to go down to his place and work with his mechanics, to build myself or, as he puts it, to build character. He thinks character comes from sweat."

He dropped his fork onto the plate with a clang that nearly made me jump in my seat.

"Sorry," he said. "I know you don't want to hear this garbage."

"That's all right. I'm just surprised, that's all," I said.

"You're surprised? You can imagine how surprised I am. Well," he said, pushing back from the table, "they leave me alone and buy me whatever I ask for. You know what I think." His eyes were now looking glassy with tears. "I think my own mother is afraid of me. She hates coming into my room. She says she can't stand looking at those specimens I have in jars and that it smells. Does my room smell?"

"No," I answered honestly.

"All she wants to do is buy me what's fashionable in clothes. That's practically the only time I go anywhere with her."

I looked down. How strange it was to hear someone with parents sound more unhappy than I was without them. Maybe he was right; maybe there were more orphans out there than I could have imagined.

"Did you ever have a boyfriend at the orphanage?" he asked softly.

I looked up and shook my head. "Everyone I meet wants to know that, too. Even Thelma asked me that," I said.

"I just wondered what kind of boys you liked," he said.

"I like boys who are honest and intelligent and caring about someone else's feelings as much as they are about their own."

"What about looks?"

"It helps if they don't have a wart on the tip of their nose or an eye in the middle of their forehead," I said, and he laughed.

"I think you're nice," he said. "I think you're nicer than most girls I know who aren't orphans. You must have good genes," he concluded. "Your mother must have been nice, too."

I looked away.

"What did she die of?" he asked. I was silent. "What was her sickness?"

"She was a manic-depressive," I shot back at him, and stood up. "She died in a mental hospital. I'd appreciate it if you wouldn't tell anyone. So, you see, my genes are not so good after all. I've got to go home," I said. "I told them I wouldn't be here that long."

"I'm sorry. I didn't mean . . ."

"It doesn't matter. Thanks for showing me your slides," I said, and headed for the door.

He came after me and took my arm to stop me before I opened the door. "I'm sorry," he said. "I didn't mean to ask so many personal questions."

"It's all right. I've got to learn how to deal with it," I said. "I'm just afraid, that's all, afraid of becoming her."

"You won't," he assured me.

"I won't? What about your belief about genes?"

"You have your father's genes, too."

"He was worse," I said, without going into it.

"Well, you have grandparents. There are lots of combinations and influences on who we are."

"When do we find out?" I asked him, my tears now bubbling at the lids.

"Find out what?"

"Who we are."

"We're always making discoveries about that," he said.

I opened the door.

"Hey," he said, stepping out alongside me.

"What?"

"Thanks for coming over." He leaned in

before I could react and kissed me quickly on the cheek.

"Why did you do that?"

He shrugged. "My genes, I guess," he said, and laughed as he stepped back inside and closed the door.

I stood there for a moment with my hand on my cheek where he had kissed it. It had happened so fast, too fast. I was disappointed.

That's the first time a boy ever did that to me, I thought as I started for home. I tried to understand the excitement that made my heart thump and brought a heat to my face. There was a movement of feelings through my body, a current that rushed in waves from my legs, through my stomach, and up around my heart, sending trickles of electricity down to the very tips of my fingers. Was this love, my first love?

My eyes were filled with his green eyes. His smile fit like a glove over mine. My brain of ten billion cells was a kaleidoscope of emotions. I felt sorry for him living like an orphan in that big, beautiful, expensive house. I wanted to go back and be with him. I wanted to hold him in my arms and tell him how to overcome the loneliness, a loneliness so strong that even all the money in the world, buying all the things he could fancy, wouldn't stop it from making his heart ache. I wanted to kiss his cheek, and then I wanted our lips to touch.

I wanted more, and what I wanted frightened me.

I closed my eyes but quickened my steps. When I opened them, I was standing in front of my new home.

I started to laugh.

It was funny. When I had left, Thelma had asked if I could see love under the microscope.

Maybe I had.

7
Seeing Stars
🐌

Falling asleep was harder than ever after I returned from Bernie's house. Thelma kept me busy with chatter about a new nighttime serial she had watched for the first time. She described the entire first episode in detail, including its settings and all its major characters. My mind wandered even as she spoke. I could hear her droning on, and I watched her animated face go through all the emotions, plucking a sigh from here, a laugh from there, and then loading up on smiles and tears before she finished with the declaration, "This is the best evening program I've seen."

I promised to watch it with her next time and then went to my room to finish my homework and organize my notebook. My stomach felt as if it had a mad bumblebee buzzing around inside. I couldn't concentrate on anything and found myself gazing out the window at the stars. I was hypnotized by the glitter and twinkle of the jeweled sky, and when I did think, I realized I had rarely spent time looking at the night sky when I lived at an orphanage. I always felt shut up, contained, and chained by bureaucratic rules and paperwork that left me feeling small and alone, just another number in some official's logbook, just another problem for society. It was better to remain unnoticed, to fold up in some corner, swallow back my tears, hide my face in books, and close the shades on my windows. There was no place for stars or for dreams in that world.

But now, after just one day at my new school, meeting new people, feeling like someone, I saw myself as reborn. I unfolded like a flower that had been stuck between the pages of the child welfare system's books. I was free to grow, to feel, to cry, and to laugh. I had a home. I had a name. I had a right to be alive and to be heard.

I couldn't help feeling like a fish out of water, however. Expressing emotions, having an opinion, and being confident around other kids my age was so new it all made me anxious and even a little afraid. Now, more than ever, I didn't want to fail. I couldn't be a disappointment to people who had invested their faith in me. I would be the best possible student, I thought. Karl would be very proud. I would help Thelma forget the ugliness and disappointments in her past, and I would give her as well as myself a reason to face a new day.

And then I would permit myself to grow into a woman. This frightened me most of all. As long as I was still seen as a little girl, I was safe, even in the orphanage. I lived in some neutral place without sex, unnoticed and unremarkable, especially by boys.

Bernie's kiss had suddenly changed all that. I felt like Sleeping Beauty. Of course, I had thoughts about sex and romance before, but somehow I never thought of myself as potentially someone's lover. I was still an observer, the little girl who sits beside the older, far more sophisticated girls and listens with wide eyes and interest to the intimate stories describing events and experiences that were still more like fantasy or science fiction but never something that would happen to me.

Now it could happen to me. I touched the place on my cheek where Bernie had kissed me, and then I rose and gazed at myself in the mirror. Was my face more mature? Would anyone look at me now and think that's a pretty young woman?

I laid out my nightgown on the bed and then went to the bathroom, brushed my teeth, took off my clothes, and returned, but

I didn't put on my nightgown. Naked, I stood before the mirror and studied my body, noting the shape of my blossoming breasts. When I turned on an angle, I saw how my body was taking shape, how the curves were softening and filling out.

My heart pounded as I looked at myself this way. I felt as if I had nudged some part of my inner self that had been hibernating. It lifted its head and smiled, welcoming my curiosity. Yes, I could hear it whisper from within, I am here, I am ready to take you on a new journey full of exciting feelings and emotions. The biological streams flowing inside will join and rush over every dry part of you. Anyone looking at your lips, your eyes, or touching your hand will see the heat and the hunger. I will make you a woman. My body was filled with the promise.

I put on my nightgown and crawled under the covers until I was snug. The soft, plush pillow was a cloud beneath my head. I was floating over the lightning and thunder of excitement I had aroused in myself, but still I tossed and turned for hours until I finally settled into a warm pocket of sleep, exhausted.

The sound of doors closing, the quick, heavy beat of footsteps, the cries coming from Thelma jerked me out of the darkness.

I listened. Either Karl or Thelma rushed up the stairs and back to the bedroom. Thelma was crying. I rose quickly and went to my door.

She was standing in the hallway with her coat on. She saw me and wiped away the tears that were streaming down her cheeks so hard they actually dripped from her chin.

"Oh, Crystal, you're up. I'm sorry we woke you, but maybe it's better."

Karl came out of the bedroom wearing his coat, too.

"What's wrong?" I asked.

"It's my mother!" Thelma cried. "She was just rushed to the emergency room. We have to go. My father is so upset he could have a stroke."

"Should I get dressed?" I asked.

"No, no," Karl said. "This could be hours and hours. You go back to sleep, and tomorrow morning, if we're not back in time, you take the bus to school. We'll be fine." He put his arm around Thelma's waist.

She reached for me and held me against her for a moment. Then the two of them hurried on.

"Isn't there anything I can do?" I called to them.

"No, no, just go back to sleep," Karl replied.

Their footsteps died away as they turned and headed for the garage.

I went to the window in my room and gazed out to watch them drive off. The street was otherwise deserted, the small patches of illumination from the lights creating a quilt of yellowish white in the darkness all the way to the corner and beyond where Karl's car turned and disappeared into the night.

The house was deadly quiet. It had all happened so fast, I felt as if I had dreamed it, especially after I crawled back under my covers and closed my eyes. It was far more difficult now to fall asleep, but shortly before the first light of day, I did. The alarm woke me. Otherwise, I would have slept through most of the morning.

I took a long shower and made myself some oatmeal. As I ate my breakfast, I looked toward the phone, hoping Karl would call before the bus came, but he didn't. I was tempted to get myself to the hospital instead of going to school, but I thought it might upset them more, so I finished getting dressed, gathered my books, and went out to wait for the bus.

Helga was already standing at the bus stop with Ashley Raymond, whose mother, Vera, was practically the only neighbor Thelma spoke to, and only because Vera was into watching soap operas, too.

"Isn't Karl taking you to school today?" Helga sang.

Ashley was about my height with light brown hair and a pair of large blue eyes too big for her small mouth and nose. She gazed at me. She always looked like a frightened doe to me. I had said about four words to her before this.

"Something happened to my grandmother last night, and he and Thelma had to rush to the hospital. They're still there," I explained.

If there was any sympathy in Helga, it was down so deep in her heart it would take an oil rig two weeks to find it. She smirked and nudged Ashley.

"Bernie will be happy. He'll have someone to sit with," she said.

"What's wrong with your grandmother?" Ashley asked quietly.

"I don't know. They rushed out too fast for me to ask questions," I said.

"I know her. She's a nice lady," Ashley said.

"Yes, she is."

"How many times did you actually even meet her?" Helga fired at me, as if I had no right to comment.

"It doesn't take long for me to know who is nice and who isn't," I said, fixing my angry eyes on her. She had to look away, but with a short, little laugh.

The bus arrived, and we boarded. I made my way to the rear, where Bernie was sitting and reading. He didn't even realize I was there until I sat beside him.

"What are you doing on the bus?" he asked with surprise.

I told him, and he shook his head.

"That's too bad."

"I hope she'll be all right," I said.

"Me, too. My mother's terrified of becoming old," he said after a moment, "but not because she might die. She's afraid of wrinkles and dry skin and gray hairs. She's had two cosmetic surgeries this year alone and" — he lowered his voice to a whisper — "a tummy tuck. You look tired." He studied me harder.

"I am."

We heard loud laughter and looked up front, where Helga and some of the other kids were talking and gazing back at us.

"When I first met Helga, I thought it would be nice to have a friend. I never really had a close friend," I said. "I almost made a big mistake."

"The woods are full of wolves," he muttered, staring at them. Then he turned to me. "I'll be your close friend if you like."

I smiled. "Okay," I said.

He went back to his reading as if looking at me was painful now. I sat with my eyes closed and shut out the chatter and the laughter until we reached the school and the beginning of my second day.

It was nearly impossible to concentrate in class. I couldn't help wondering and worrying. At lunchtime, Bernie escorted me to the pay phone and waited as I called home. The phone rang and rang until Karl's voice came on from the answering machine, asking the caller to leave a name and number, time of call, and a brief statement of the call's purpose. It sounded more like the message at an office than at a house. I left my name.

"No one's home yet," I told Bernie.

He thought a moment. "Well, that's good. Whatever's being done for her is still being done."

Bernie was a little reluctant about returning to the cafeteria to have lunch with me, but he agreed, and we sat together at a small table toward the rear. From this position, we could see that many other students were looking at us and talking about us.

"It feels like we're in a fishbowl," Bernie quipped. He ate and read his science book, pausing occasionally to talk about something from our class work.

I began to wonder if his kissing me was something I had imagined. He showed so little interest in me and actually jumped in his seat when our arms grazed each other. Other girls who had boyfriends sat closer to them, some practically on their laps, laughing and talking to each other as if there were no one else in the cafeteria. When the bell rang to end the lunch hour, they walked off holding hands. Bernie and I walked side by side but clutching our books as if they were life vests and we were on the deck of a sinking ship. I saw from the way some of the other girls looked at us, whispering and giggling, that we were already the subject of very nasty jokes.

My next class was nearly half over when the speaker on the wall clicked and a voice requested that my teacher send me to the principal's office. Everyone looked at me as I rose and left the room. The principal's secretary told me to take a seat and wait. A few minutes later, the door opened, and there was Karl with Mr. Nissen. I didn't need to hear any words. The expressions on their faces told all.

"I didn't want to take you out of school, Crystal, but Thelma is asking for you and thinks you should come right home with me," he said.

"Of course." I didn't know what else to say.

"Don't worry about your homework. I'll see to it that your assignments are sent to the house," Mr. Nissen said.

"She won't be out that long," Karl assured him.

"Take whatever time she needs," Mr. Nissen said. "Please give Mrs. Morris my sympathies."

I realized I had left my briefcase, books, and notebooks on my desk and had to hurry back to get them. Everyone turned my way when I entered and went to my desk. Our teacher paused. I gathered up my books and put them into the briefcase quickly.

"What are you doing, Crystal?" Mr. Saddler asked.

I went up to him. It wasn't the sort of thing I wanted to shout out. "I'm sorry, Mr. Saddler, but I have to go right home. My grandmother has died."

"Oh," he said. He looked awkward and confused, like someone who had stepped onto ice. "Of course. I'm sorry."

He waited for me to leave before he started the class again. As I walked toward the door, I looked over at Bernie. He nodded at me, his face as tight and as serious as a doctor giving his patient's loved ones hard news. I left quickly, the door closing behind me softly, and then I hurried down the corridor to where Karl was waiting. We walked out together, neither of us saying a word until we were in his car.

"What happened?" I finally asked.

"The doctor said she didn't have much more than fifteen percent of her heart muscle working by the time she was brought in. They did the best they could. She lasted longer than they thought she would. Thelma says that was because of you."

"Me?"

"She says her mother wanted to stay with us longer so she could see you grow up in our family. It's what she believes, and it's what makes it sadder for her," he said. "I'm sorry that you've had such a hard beginning with us," he added.

"How's Grandpa?" I asked.

Karl shook his head. "Fragile. I don't know how he is going to last alone. As sick as she was, Thelma's mother took good care of him," he said.

"What's going to happen to him?"

"As soon as I can, I'll start looking for a good adult residency for him. We can't take him in with us. We don't have the room," he added.

If I hadn't come to live with them, they

would have the room, I thought. I felt just terrible about it. Would Grandpa resent me? Would Thelma?

"I could share my room with him," I suggested.

"Of course you can't," Karl said. "Besides, we can't give him the attention he's going to need. Thelma's not good at looking after sick folk. If I get a cold, she panics. Don't you get sick," he warned. "Those damn shows put all sorts of ideas in her head about this illness and that. Mention a pain, and she'll give you an episode on *Community Hospital* that fits it. No, don't worry about Grandpa. I'll see to him," Karl promised. "With his insurance and retirement pension, he can afford something decent."

That didn't make me feel any better about it, but I didn't say anything else. When we entered the house, I saw a glow coming from the television set, yet as we drew closer, I didn't hear anything.

"We're back," Karl called, and stopped in the doorway.

Thelma was sitting in her favorite chair, staring at the silent television screen, her face streaked with tears. She looked up at me, and her shoulders shook.

"Poor Grandma," she said. "She wanted to have a grandchild so much, and just when

she had one, she goes and dies. It's so unfair.
It's like . . . like the electricity going off just
at an important part in one of my programs."

"I'm sorry," I said, certain that her
mother's death meant more to her than a
power outage. She was just upset. "She was
very nice. I was hoping to get to know her a
lot more."

"You poor dear. Now you have no grandmother," she cried.

I didn't know whether or not I should run
to her side and hug her. She turned from me
and stared at the television screen.

"Do you want something to eat, Thelma?"
Karl asked. He turned to me. "She hasn't
eaten a thing all day."

"I'll make you something, Mom."

She smiled through her tears. "Maybe just
some tea and toast with a little jelly," she
said. "And then come and sit beside me for a
while."

Karl and I went to the kitchen and got her
tea and toast together on a tray that I started
to bring back to her.

"Do you think you'll be all right here?" he
asked me before I returned to Thelma. "I
have to stop at the office for a few minutes."

"Yes, we'll be fine," I said.

He told Thelma what he was doing, but

she didn't respond. She didn't turn from the silent screen until I brought the tray to her and set it up on the coffee table. I watched her nibble the toast and sip the tea, her eyes shifting with the movements of the actors on the surface of the picture tube. Keeping the sound off appeared to be her gesture of mourning.

"The funeral is the day after tomorrow," she said during the commercial. Her eyes still remained fixed on the screen, as if she was afraid that if she didn't keep looking at it she would fall apart. "Karl has everything arranged."

"Where's Grandpa?" I asked.

"He's home with some of their friends. People about their age. He's more comfortable at home," she continued. She nibbled some more of her toast and sipped her tea. "When you lose someone you love, you're better off being where everything is familiar, doing the things you're accustomed to doing. Grandma wouldn't want me to miss my show," she added when the program continued.

I stared at her, and then I looked at the set. The characters were obviously screaming at each other in an argument of some kind. What good was it watching with the sound off? Thelma shook her head as if she could hear the words anyway.

"Isn't it better if we just talk, Mom?" I asked softly.

"Talk? About what? Not about Grandma," she said, shaking her head vigorously. "I don't want to talk about her dying. She wasn't supposed to die," she said firmly, as if someone had rewritten a script. "She wanted to watch her granddaughter grow up. I told Karl we should adopt a child a long time ago. We shouldn't have waited to get you. Now look at what's happened. It doesn't fit," she said. "It all doesn't fit."

"We can't plan our lives like a soap opera is planned, Mom. We don't have that power." I wanted to add "yet," because I believed that someday science would crack all the mysteries of genetics and a great deal about our lives would be predetermined, but this wasn't the time to bring that up, I thought.

She shook her head. "I don't want to talk about it," she said. "It's too sad." She looked at the television set. "You're never home for this one. I told you about it, though. This is the one with the daughter who has AIDS. Her parents are blaming each other. See?"

I looked down at the floor. I was far from an expert on mourning the death of a loved one. Until now, I had no loved ones. No death had ever touched me deeply. Even when I read about my real mother, it was more like reading a story about someone else. I didn't have her face in my mind, her voice in my memory. I couldn't recall her touching me, kissing me, speaking to me. I had no father, no grandparents, no relatives' deaths to mourn. I never even had a close friend or someone at one of the orphanages with whom I had grown so close that I was saddened by their passing or departure.

Being alone had its advantages, I thought. I could only mourn myself. I need only be sorry about myself.

Helga was right in a sense. I hadn't known my new grandmother long enough to feel as deeply about her death as most grandchildren would feel about the deaths of their beloved grandparents. Shouldn't I be crying? Shouldn't I be in a corner somewhere, sobbing? I wasn't sure about my own feelings and actions. I wasn't even sure I should be criticizing Thelma for what she was doing. Maybe it was wrong to take away her distractions. Maybe it was wrong to force her to face the reality of her mother's death.

She finished her toast and smiled at me. "I'm glad you're here with me," she said. "I'm sorry you're missing class, though."

"It's all right. I'll get the work sent home. Bernie will probably bring it over later," I conjectured.

"That's nice. You can sit closer to me," she suggested.

I moved closer, and she reached out and took my hand. Then she turned back to the silent television screen. I watched her face. The shadows and the light bounced off it, leaving her with a smile and then with a look of pity or disgust. Occasionally, she sighed or smacked her lips in criticism. I widened my eyes in astonishment. It was truly as though she knew what they were saying.

I wanted to ask her how she could watch the show this way. I wanted to point out that the sound was off, but I couldn't get myself to do it. It was like telling someone what they saw wasn't real, that it was only make-believe.

Thelma needed make-believe, I thought. Who was I to tell her she couldn't have it or she shouldn't believe?

I let her hold my hand tighter and sat beside her in silence.

It was the way Karl found us when he returned.

8
Truth or Dare

After dinner, Ashley and her mother, Vera, came to offer condolences to Thelma. Ashley had all the homework I had missed at the end of the day, even from the classes Bernie and I shared. She told me he had given it to her on the bus. I felt let down because I had hoped he would bring it over himself. Sometimes my eyes were like windows with the shades up. Ashley took one look at me and saw the disappointment.

"Bernie's really very shy," she said. "I'm probably one of the few people he speaks to once in a while, and that's only because I never make fun of him. I think he's brilliant."

"He *is* brilliant," I said. I took Ashley to my room while her mother visited with Thelma and Karl.

"What was it like living in an orphanage?" she asked as soon as we were alone. Was there anyone who looked at me and didn't wonder about that? "Were the adults cruel to you?"

"It's not like an orphanage in a Dickens novel," I said.

"What's a Dickens novel?"

"Charles Dickens? *A Christmas Carol? Tale of Two Cities? Hard Times?* Doesn't any of that ring a bell?" I followed with a frown.

"Oh yeah," she said, but she still had a blank look on her face.

"What I mean is, it isn't like living with your own family, having your own room, but you're not made to shovel coal or wash floors, and you don't have to wear rags and eat gruel."

"Gruel? Ugh."

"You don't have to eat it," I emphasized. "I wasn't happy there, but I wasn't being tortured."

She nodded. "Helga says girls who live in orphanages lose their virginity faster," she commented.

"What? Where does she get the right to make such a stupid statement? How does she know about girls who live in orphanages?" I demanded.

Ashley shrugged. "It's just what she says."

"Well, for your information and for hers, it isn't so." I saw the way Ashley was staring at me. "I haven't lost mine," I added. "It sounds to me like Helga's lost hers."

Ashley laughed. "Sometimes I think she

wishes she did. The way she chases after some of the boys, I mean. She told me she would let Todd Philips do anything he wanted if he took her out."

"She said that?"

"Uh-huh." Ashley nodded, those big eyes even bigger.

"She might be disappointed," I muttered.

"Why?" Ashley asked quickly. "I thought that was the most wonderful thing that could happen."

"Who told you that?"

She shrugged again. "I just listen to what the others say, especially those who've had sex and brag about it in the girls' room. They make it sound wonderful."

"Well, I wouldn't really know . . . I've never . . ." I was about to tell Ashley I'd never even been kissed, but I didn't really trust that she would keep that information to herself. "I've never been one to kiss and tell," I said instead.

We talked a while about movie star kisses and who we thought kissed best, and I could tell that Ashley was as curious about what it would be like to kiss a boy as I was.

After Ashley left, I began my homework, eager to think about something other than boys. Before Thelma and Karl went to sleep, he returned to my room.

"Maybe you should go to school tomorrow, Crystal. There's really no point in your sitting around here all day."

"Won't Thelma need me?" I asked.

He thought a moment. "She'll sleep a lot," he said.

"Just the same, I think I'll stay nearby," I offered.

He smiled. "Okay. You're probably right. It's nice to have someone else in the house who cares about her," he added. I thought he might come farther into my room and kiss me good night, but he stood there, nodding a moment longer, and then he said good night and closed the door.

It takes time to become father and daughter, I thought, and with some it takes a lot longer.

Thelma didn't rise as early as she ordinarily did the next morning. Karl brought her some breakfast and then asked me to look in on her after a while. He said he was off to check on Grandpa before going to work. I offered to go along, but he said he would have to bring me home afterward and that would add too much time to his being away from his office.

"You'd be surprised how the work piles up on me," he said.

"Won't they understand at the company?" I asked him.

"No one supervises me more than I supervise myself," Karl replied. He nodded, his eyes intense. "That's the secret to being successful, Crystal: demand more of yourself than others do. You're your own best critic, understand?"

"Yes," I said.

He left, and I sat quietly, reading ahead in my history book, imagining what the next assignment would be. A little over an hour later, Thelma appeared in the living-room doorway. Her hair was disheveled, her eyes bloodshot. Her skin was ashen. She looked as if she had aged years in one night. She had a half dozen tissues clutched in her hand. Still in her nightgown, she shuffled across the room in what looked like Karl's slippers and plopped with a deep sigh into her favorite chair.

"Would you like something, Mom?" I asked.

She shook her head. "I don't like thinking about my mother," she said softly. "It hurts. I wanted to go to the phone to call her this morning like I usually do before *Shadows at Dawn*. I actually lifted the receiver before I remembered she was gone."

She sniffled and wiped her eyes. "What can I do?" she cried.

"We could talk, Mom. Sometimes it feels

better when you talk about what's bothering you," I said. My counselors always used that line on me when I was at the orphanages. There really was some truth to it, however.

Thelma stared at me a moment. "I can't," she said, shaking her head. "Every time I think about her, I start to cry. I can't. It's better not to think." She snapped up the television remote as if it were a bottle of pills promising relief.

She turned on the television set and flipped through the channels until she found a program she liked. This time, she left the sound on, too. She began to react to what she was watching, smiling, laughing, looking concerned. I had begun to read again when I suddenly heard her say, "I dread going to the funeral tomorrow. Why do we have to have funerals?"

"It's our last chance to say good-bye," I said, even though I had never been to a funeral before and the very thought of going put almost as much apprehension in me.

"I don't want to say good-bye." She moaned. "I hate good-byes. I wish I could just sit here and watch it on television. That way, if it got too sad, I could turn it off, turn to something else."

"My psychologist at the orphanage always told me it's worse to avoid your problems,

Mom. It's better to face them and deal with them," I said softly.

She stared at me a moment and then smiled. "You're so smart," she said. "We're lucky to have you. I will have something to eat. Could you make me some scrambled eggs and toast?"

"Sure," I said, getting up quickly.

"And some coffee," she called as I started out. Then she turned back to her program.

Thelma remained there most of the day, getting up only to go to the bathroom. I made her lunch as well. She didn't talk unless she had a comment to make about something she was watching. The highlight of her day began when her first soap was on. After that, I might as well have gone to school. Karl called to see how she was and to tell me that he had someone taking care of Grandpa. I told him what Thelma was doing.

"Maybe she's better off," he said.

"I'm not doing much," I complained. I wanted to add that he'd been right. I should have gone to school.

"You're there. That's something," he said. "She probably wouldn't eat anything otherwise."

He was right about that, but I still felt more like a maid than a daughter. I wanted

134

to talk. I wanted to hear Thelma tell stories about her mother, about what it was like being her daughter, the things they had shared, their precious moments, all that she would miss. I wanted to feel that I was part of a family and not back in the orphanage with strangers.

When Thelma started to cry about what was happening to a character on her program, I got up and went to my room. How could she care so much more about make-believe people? Was it because it felt safer? The program ended, and you didn't have to think about them anymore? Was that it? But Thelma seemed to think about the characters constantly, not just when the show was on. I couldn't make any sense of it.

A little while later, the doorbell rang. It was Ashley and her mother again, only this time Bernie was with them.

"Hi," I said, smiling mostly for Bernie's benefit.

"How's she doing?" Mrs. Raymond asked.

"She's been watching television, trying not to think about it," I said.

"I don't blame her," Mrs. Raymond said.

"We brought all your homework," Ashley said. "And Bernie came along to help explain anything new."

"Thanks."

I stepped back, and everyone entered. Mrs. Raymond went to see Thelma, and I took Ashley and Bernie to my room. Bernie opened the math book and began to talk about the new problems immediately. I listened and nodded when he asked if I understood.

Ashley sat on my bed and watched us work. When his explanations ended, Bernie sat at my computer.

"So when is the funeral?" he asked.

"In the morning. There won't be many people there. Karl's father isn't able to travel, and his brother in Albany can't get away. His younger brother is at sea. None of Thelma's cousins are coming. Some of my grandparents' older friends will be there."

"And my mother will be there," Ashley said quickly. "She won't let me. She says I have to go to school."

"She's right," Bernie said. "School is more important. Funerals are really unnecessary."

"Unnecessary? How can you say that?" Ashley asked.

"When someone dies, it's over. There's no point in wasting any more time about it."

"That's a horrible thing to say," Ashley declared. "You have to pay respect."

"To what? The person's gone. You're better off saying good-bye to a picture," he remarked. "I hated going to my grand-father's funeral. There was a big party after-ward, full of people who really never knew him. It was just an excuse for a party."

"We're not having anything afterward," I said.

"Good," Bernie said.

"That's cruel, Bernie Felder," Ashley charged.

"I'm just being realistic," he said. "When you die, you return to some form of energy, and that energy goes into something else. That's it."

"What else?" Ashley asked, her eyebrows hoisted so high they were practically in the middle of her forehead.

"I don't know. Maybe . . . a plant or a bug."

"A bug! Crystal, you don't believe that, do you?"

"I don't know what I believe," I said. "Sometimes I imagine my real mother is with me, her spirit, but then I think that's silly."

"It's not silly. It's beautiful," Ashley said. "I'm not going to be any bug, Bernie Felder. Maybe you are."

"Maybe," Bernie said casually.

"You don't care?"

"Why should I care? I won't know anything different," he said, and Ashley groaned.

"I swear," she said. "Scientists are the most boring people. I hate the subject, especially experiments with all those smelly chemicals and dead worms. Experiments make me sick."

"I bet I can think of an experiment you'd like. How about an experiment to find out what kind of kisses we like best?" I asked her, thinking she'd call my bluff.

"Crystal!" she said, shifting her eyes to Bernie.

"What kind of experiment?" he asked excitedly.

I made up an experiment that was almost like a contest — judging the best kiss. He listened and nodded without laughing. Ashley's face turned pink when I turned to ask if she was willing to join in.

"Interesting," Bernie said. "I don't see how it's really scientific . . ." He thought a moment and then nodded at me. "But I'd like to be part of it."

"Good," I said.

"What?" Ashley cried. "Crystal, I thought you were just kidding!"

"Don't be chicken, Ashley," Bernie said. "It's not like we're doing anything serious — just kissing."

"But I don't want to be judged against Crystal . . . I've never kissed a boy before!" she cried, turning to me for help.

I wanted to make Ashley feel better and tell her I'd never kissed a boy, either, but I wanted to keep my inexperience from Bernie. "You'll have to swear to keep this a secret. You know what someone like Helga would do if she found out."

Ashley looked at Bernie and then at me apprehensively.

"You're not going to get pregnant or anything like that," Bernie promised. "You're just going to discover more about yourself, and it will be knowledge that will make you wiser, stronger. That's the purpose and power of knowledge."

"He's right," I said. "Okay?"

"Maybe," Ashley said. "I'll see," she added cautiously, but I could tell she was almost as intrigued about it as we were.

Bernie volunteered to set up what he called the control procedures. He said we would be more secure if we met at his house. With some reluctance, Ashley agreed.

"This is like playing doctor," she whispered to me when we left my room.

"Did you ever do that?" I asked. She shifted her eyes to Bernie and then to me.

"No," she said. "Did you?"

"No, but I wanted to," I admitted.

She took a small breath and said, "Me, too."

Then she hurried to join her mother and leave, frightened by her own confession.

The funeral the next day was simple and took less time than I expected, probably because Karl had everything so well organized. After the church service, the undertaker's car took us to the cemetery. Grandpa looked very fragile, clinging to the arm of a special-duty nurse Karl had hired. Thelma seemed like someone drugged, right from the moment she woke and dressed. Whenever I looked at her, her eyes were unfocused and distant. It was as if they were open but shut off, and she was not seeing or listening to anything that went on around her. She had retreated into her own mind. Maybe she was replaying one of her television programs.

Karl led her about, moving everyone along gracefully and efficiently. Some of the people from his office attended the church service, but at the cemetery, there were only two other elderly couples who had been friends with Thelma's mother, her father and the nurse, Thelma, Karl, me, Ashley's mother, and the minister.

It really wasn't a good day for a funeral. It

was too warm and bright with a nearly cloudless sky, the blue more like turquoise. At the cemetery, the air was filled with the aroma of freshly cut grass. Birds flitted from tree to tree, and squirrels frolicked about the tombstones as if the entire cemetery had been created for their sole pleasure.

I couldn't help wondering what my real mother's funeral must have been like. I imagined myself finding out where she was buried and going to visit her grave someday. What would I say? Who would hear it, anyway? Was Bernie right? Was there nothing left of us afterward, or did something precious linger, something we didn't understand, couldn't understand?

On the way home, Thelma finally spoke. She said, "Poor Mom. I hope she's not alone."

That was what Thelma was most afraid of, I thought, being alone. For years, her television programs had provided her with the families and friends she never had in real life. They had filled her life with distraction and kept her from thinking about her own loneliness. Karl thought adopting me would help, but I still didn't feel I was giving them much, and I certainly didn't feel we were a family. At least, not what I thought a family would be like.

Grandpa came home with us to eat, but he fell asleep in his chair after having only a few bites. He looked as if he had shrunken and withered with his sorrow. I hoped in my secret heart that someday, somehow, I would find someone who loved me as much. That, I thought, was the true antidote to loneliness, the best cure of all.

Two days later, Grandpa had a stroke and was taken to the hospital. He didn't die, but he was so incapacitated Karl had to arrange for him to be placed in permanent institutional care. Thelma couldn't stand the thought of visiting him in such surroundings.

"Why do we have to grow old?" She moaned. "It's not fair. Elena doesn't look a day older than she did when I first started to watch *Shadows of Forever*. We should all live inside a television program."

Karl shook his head helplessly and went back to his business magazine. I returned to my homework, and our lives continued as if we were three shadows searching for a way to become whole again.

We visited Karl's father, but it wasn't any more successful a visit than the first one. He grew impatient with Thelma's sad demeanor and Karl's criticism of his lifestyle and went off to be with his friends. A few days later,

Karl's brother Stuart finally drove over from Albany to meet me and offer his sympathies to Thelma. He was taller and thinner than Karl, but he had colder eyes and a hard, chiseled face on which a smile settled only fleetingly. He asked me questions about school but seemed uncomfortable when I spoke to him and looked at him. I noticed he avoided my eyes and didn't look directly at me when he spoke to me.

After Stuart left, Karl revealed that his brother had almost become a monk. He said it was still possible that one day he would.

"People make him nervous," he said. "He cherishes solitude."

"How does he work as a salesman, then?" I asked. "Salesmen have to meet people."

"He does most of his work over the telephone. He's a telemarketer."

I was disappointed. I had been hoping my uncle would be friendlier and more fun. I had even imagined going to visit him in Albany. I complained about it to Bernie and Ashley the day after.

Ever since we had decided to be part of an experiment, Ashley began to hang around with me, and consequently with Bernie, more at school. She sat with us at lunch.

"My biggest hope was that I would become part of a real family," I said, "and have

143

relatives with parties and birthdays, anniversaries and weddings. All of it. Sometimes I feel more alone than I was at the orphanage."

Ashley looked very sad for me, her eyes full of pain, but Bernie sat musing for a moment as if I had brought up a topic from science class.

"Family is overrated," he suddenly declared with that confident, really arrogant air in which he answered questions and made statements in class. "It's a myth created by greeting-card companies. People are too into themselves to be that sort of thing anymore."

"That's terrible. My family isn't into themselves," Ashley protested.

Bernie's eyebrows nearly touched as he creased his lips. "Your father is always traveling. You told us that yourself a few days ago, and your mother is terrified of becoming old, just like mine. Face it," he said, nodding at me, "we're not so much different from Crystal. No one really listens to us. Usually, we're in the way. At best, we're a mild annoyance."

"I'm not!"

"We're all orphans," Bernie muttered. "We're all searching for something that's not there."

"That's not true. You don't believe that, Crystal, do you?"

"I don't know," I said. "I don't want to believe that, but I don't know."

Ashley looked terribly distraught, ready to get up and run away. Then Bernie leaned in to whisper. "Let's not worry about all that. Let's get to our experiment. I'm ready," he said. "My house tonight, about seven-thirty. Okay?"

I looked at Ashley. Her face suddenly changed from dark to light, her eyes shifting nervously as she looked at me and then at Bernie.

"Fine," I said. "Ashley?"

"Okay," she said in a small voice. "But I'm not an orphan."

Bernie laughed. I hadn't heard him laugh that hard before. It brought a smile to my face, and that made Ashley smile, too.

Across the cafeteria, the other students who had been looking at us with disdain were now suddenly full of curiosity about us.

But nowhere near as much as we were about ourselves.

9

In the Name of Science

🍄

"This is a graph," Bernie began, holding up a grid. "There's one for each of us."

Ashley and I sat on two chairs in his room while he stood and lectured. Ashley said it felt as if she were back in school. I asked her to be patient.

"This will be session one," he continued, closing and opening his eyes with annoyance. "We will do the same things each session and rate our reactions to them on a scale of one to ten, ten being the most intense. Our objective is to determine how kissing affects us, which kisses we like best, and so on. Understand?" he asked. He did sound and look like Mr. Friedman, our science teacher.

"No," Ashley said, shaking her head. "It sounds like gobbledygook. What does a graph have to do with kissing?"

"The graph doesn't have anything to do with it. It's just a way of recording reactions scientifically." Bernie sighed with frustration. He looked at me. "You see why I could never be a teacher?"

Bernie shook his head, took a deep breath, and returned to his chart.

"We'll meet here every night over the next week or so," he said.

"I still don't understand what we're doing," Ashley whined.

"Ultimately, we're going to see which kinds of kisses we like best, dry, quick pecks or long, wet ones," Bernie said a bit cruelly. "You have thought about kissing a boy before, right? Just pretend I'm whatever boy you're in love with this week, and plant one on me."

Ashley sucked in her breath and held it. She looked as if she might explode. Her eyes bulged. She looked from me to Bernie and then started to shake her head.

"I won't do that," she said. She kept shaking her head.

"You're not going to sit there and tell us you've never thought about kissing a boy?" He was getting exasperated. "It's natural to think about it."

She couldn't get any redder, I thought, and I felt myself blushing as well. All this talk about kissing was making me as nervous as Ashley.

"It's very important that we're honest with one another," Bernie emphasized. "In science, honesty is essential. We can't hide truth, and we can't pretend. No one here is going to laugh or make fun of anyone else, either. We're serious, and we're going to be adult about it, right, Crystal?"

"Yes," I said, surprised myself at how clinical Bernie made it all seem. It didn't even sound sexy or mysterious. Which is how I always dreamed it would be.

"Why is he the one telling us everything we have to do?" Ashley complained.

"You asked me to help with this experiment, and I've done it," Bernie said.

"I didn't ask. Crystal and I were curious about kissing, and you butted in, right, Crystal?"

"Yes, but we need Bernie's help."

"You're going to do this?" she asked.

"Yes," I said, looking at Bernie, who seemed more determined and purposeful than ever. "I'm very interested, and I know we'll learn a lot more about ourselves."

She glued her huge eyes to my face for a moment.

"Well?" Bernie demanded.

"All right," Ashley said. "If Crystal's going to do it, I'll try."

"Good," Bernie said. He walked over to his door and locked it. Then he went to the windows and closed all the blinds tightly.

Ashley's eyes followed his every move. He handed each of us a graph.

"The numbers at the side correspond to the activities," he explained. "It will be easier if we just refer to them by their numbers. On the top as you see are the dates, beginning with today. As long as we keep this scientific, we'll do fine," he added.

He went to a cabinet under his wall of shelves and opened it.

"What's that?" Ashley asked before he had a chance to explain.

"It's a digital blood-pressure cup, and it also records pulse."

"Where did you get that?" she asked, as if it were some forbidden fruit.

"You can get these anywhere, Ashley. They sell them in drugstores. It's no big deal," Bernie said. "Now, when you're aroused," he continued in his scientist's voice, "your blood pressure should rise and your pulse, of course, will quicken. Let's take our blood pressures and pulses right now before we do anything else, so we'll know what to consider normal and what not, okay? Who's first?"

"I'll start," I said, and Bernie fit the cup around my arm. When I was done, he measured Ashley.

"You must be a little nervous," he said. "I

149

wouldn't expect your pressure to be this high."

He did his own, which was as low as mine.

"How come you two are so calm?" Ashley asked suspiciously. "Aren't you nervous, Crystal?"

"No." It was true. Now that we were ready to begin, I was more anxious than nervous to find out what it felt like to be kissed.

She looked skeptical. "Now what?" she asked.

Bernie sat across from us, crossed his legs, and gazed at his notes.

"Now, we should kiss. Ashley, you want to go first?" he asked.

Ashley popped up from her chair like a jack-in-the-box. She fumbled with the door lock and ran out before Bernie could ask her what she was doing. Moments later, we heard the front door slam.

Bernie and I looked at each other.

"I don't think she was quite ready for this," he said with a smile.

"I think you did all that just to get rid of her," I said, finally beginning to understand why he had been so clinical.

His eyes met mine as he tried to hide the truth.

"I knew she wouldn't be ready. Why waste time with her?"

"Why did you want to do this?" I asked. "Remember," I quickly followed, "honesty is essential in science."

He started to smile and stopped to put on his serious face again. "I've had different feelings about you, different from what I've felt about other girls, and I wanted to understand why," he explained.

"So this is still an experiment?"

"Yes," he said. "What else could it be?"

I wanted to say it could be love; it could be romance. I wanted to say that maybe we shouldn't dissect our feelings, that maybe that would destroy them, but I didn't say anything. I didn't want to drive him away, and there was an excitement that started as a small trembling in my legs and moved up my spine until my heartbeat quickened.

"Should we get on with this?" Bernie asked. His eyes were full of anticipation and hope.

Once, at the orphanage, I had caught a girl named Marsha Benjamin in a very passionate embrace with a boy much older than she. His name was Glen Fraser, and I remember being afraid of him, afraid of the way he looked at me. I was too young to understand why at the time, but when I saw him and Marsha kissing, his hand under her skirt, his body moving roughly against hers, forcing

151

her to turn so that he could move between her legs, I gasped first in fear and then in astonishment. I started to run away but stopped, unable to shut my curious eyes. The truth was, I was fascinated with Marsha's face, with the way she let her head fall back, with her small moans, and especially with her hands, first trying to stop it all from happening and then, suddenly, apparently filled with uncontrollable excitement, pulling her hand away from his to hold him behind his neck as if she were clinging to him for dear life.

He turned and saw me standing there, watching them. He didn't get angry. He smiled coolly and said, "There's room for one more."

I ran. I ran so hard and fast someone would have thought I was being pursued by a monster. Years later, I would think the monster was inside me. I wanted to conquer it, to be unafraid, and I thought that would never happen until I was fulfilled and loved by someone I could feel good about. Now I wondered if Bernie could be that person.

"Yes," I replied finally, "let's go on with it."

Bernie smiled, and then, as if he read my thoughts, he said, "We'll go slowly, of course, and if either of us is uncomfortable, we'll stop immediately. That would only ruin the experiment, anyway."

"Fine," I said, swallowing back the lump of nervousness that tried to rise in my throat.

Bernie walked over and began to kiss me. I closed my eyes and let my mind drift, but I could feel my heart pounding crazily, and I worried that Bernie could feel it, too. I pulled away, and Bernie slowly dropped his hands from my shoulders.

Bernie lifted his eyes slowly and gazed at me.

"How do you feel?" he asked.

"Very nervous," I said.

"You're the bravest girl I ever met. I didn't think you would do this," he confessed, and I thought I heard a faint quiver of nervousness in his voice.

"I told you," I said, trying to sound brave, "I'm as interested as you."

He nodded.

"What do we do next?" I asked.

"Why don't we try a French kiss? You know, with our tongues?" he said. "You tell me everything that's happening to you, and I'll do the same, okay?"

I nodded. I began to wish I'd left with Ashley, but I knew it was too late to turn back now. Besides, I was curious about

Bernie and the way his kiss had made me feel.

"Ready?"

"Yes," I said. I looked up at the ceiling and then at him, and we both stood there.

His eyes drank me in from head to toe. I had never had a boy look at me the way Bernie was doing. It made my head swim.

"My heart is pounding," he said. He began to walk around me. "I'm nervous, and I'm afraid I might do something wrong," he admitted. He sounded like someone reporting from outer space — as if I weren't in the same room as him, experiencing the same feelings and emotions.

"Me, too." I wanted to be honest about my reactions, for the sake of the experiment, of course

"What?"

"Everything you said," I said, my voice cracking, my eyes closing as he walked around me. I could feel his breath on my neck. A moment later, he was in front of me again, only inches away.

"I'm going to close my eyes," he said, "and then I'm going to try this French kiss thing, okay?"

He closed his eyes and kissed me.

I wasn't too sure I liked this kind of kiss. I felt as if I could tell what Bernie had had for dinner. I'd seen kids kiss in school like this, and they seemed to enjoy it, so I decided to try to like it. After a while, my heart began pounding stronger, and my hands started to feel sweaty. This time, though, it was Bernie who stopped our kiss.

"Wow." He shook his head as if he were trying to clear the fog out. "*Now* I see what all the hype is for."

"Um . . . yeah, me, too." I couldn't help but wonder if kissing all boys felt this nice.

"I think we should stop for tonight, but I definitely want to try this again. As long as we keep it experimental, of course," he added.

"Experimental . . . of course," I answered, trying to keep the disappointment out of my voice. I was never one of those girls who got all dreamy when they talked about boys and kissing, but I never thought it would be cold or clinical, either.

"I wonder if Ashley's going to tell her other friends about this," he said.

"I'll make sure she doesn't."

"They'll make up stories about us anyway," he said, holding his eyes on mine. "They probably already have."

"Probably," I agreed.

There was a long moment of silence between us. To me, it was as if we had fantasized the kisses we'd shared. It had all been so fast it was one blurry memory. Only the graph in my hands with my comments confirmed that I hadn't been dreaming.

"I'd better get home," I said.

"I'll walk you." He smiled at my surprise. "I don't think I could do any reading, concentrate on anything, or go to sleep for a while anyway," he explained.

I laughed to hide what I was feeling, the same excitement still echoing in my body.

He opened the door, and we started out. We were almost to the door when we heard someone call from the living room.

"My mother," Bernie said under his breath.

A very elegant-looking woman, dressed as if she was on her way to an important ball or just returning from one, came toward us, her long diamond-studded earrings swinging from her lobes. Her styled hair was nearly platinum, the strands so perfectly shaped I wondered if she was wearing a wig. She was tall, with an hourglass figure that seemed held together by wires and pins. When she stepped out of the shadows and drew closer, I saw that her face was so free of wrinkles it looked like a mask. Her temples were stiff, pulling back on her eyes as if her skin had shrunk. Her nose was small, but the nostrils were a little too large. The puffiness in her lips made her smile seem painful. It was more of a grimace.

The fingers of her left hand were full of rings. She looked like a walking jewelry store with her diamond necklace, hairpin, and bracelets. I thought she might have taken a bath in expensive perfume. The scent arrived days before she did.

"Who's this, Bernard?" she asked.

"A friend," he said quickly.

"Why don't you introduce me? You've never had a friend over before, and especially not a female friend," she said, her eyes fixed on me.

"This is Crystal," he said. "Crystal, my mother."

"Hello," I said quickly.

"Crystal who?" she asked without replying.

"Crystal Morris," Bernie said. "She was just going home."

"Morris? Which Morris is that? Charlie Morris from the advertisement agency?"

"No," Bernie said. "I'm walking her home." He practically lunged at the front door and opened it.

"It's nice to meet you," his mother said as I started after him. "It's about time Bernie brought someone home," she added. She looked as if she could shatter her face by changing expression too rapidly. I gazed back at her once and then hurried to catch up to Bernie, who was already out of the house.

He closed the door behind me and nearly jogged down the walkway.

"Maybe we shouldn't have run out like that, Bernie," I said, catching up. He walked faster.

"All she wants me to do is have girlfriends, listen to rock music, and dress like some teenage movie or television star," he muttered. "Look at her," he said, stopping and gazing back at his house. "If that was your mother, would you want anyone to meet her? She just likes to embarrass me." He started walking again. " 'It's about time you brought someone home,' " he mimicked. " 'Especially a female friend.' "

"She's probably just worried about you," I offered.

"No, she's not. She's worried about herself, about what it will look like if I'm not a so-called normal young man. Let's not talk about it. It just gets me angry," he said.

We walked silently until we reached my house. It was an overcast night, and there was a chill in the air. Our breath could be seen in vague little puffs. Neither of us was really dressed warmly enough.

"You hold onto these," he said at the door. He handed me the graphs. I hadn't noticed them clutched in his hand.

"We should probably just leave them in your room," I said.

He shook his head. "Sometimes, when I'm in school, she goes into my room and searches it, looking for something bizarre. I deliberately left a dissected frog reeking from formaldehyde on the table one morning, and she stayed away for a while, but she still spies on me from time to time. I don't want her finding these papers," he said. "She would never understand."

"Okay," I said, taking them. I was certain Karl and Thelma wouldn't understand, either, but I wasn't ready for our experiments to end.

"Good night." He hesitated. "I really enjoyed our experiment," he said. "I'm looking forward to tomorrow." He turned to leave and then stepped back to kiss me quickly on the cheek again.

I stood there with my hand on my cheek, watching him disappear up the sidewalk. Then I went inside, my brain whirling, a potpourri of emotions making me dizzy. Karl was still up, but Thelma had gone to bed.

"She was very tired tonight. She kept falling asleep in her chair, so I got her to go to bed," he explained. "How are you doing?"

"Okay," I said.

"Good. Well, the worst is over," he declared. "Now we'll return to a normal life."

What is a normal life? I wanted to ask. Was it a life full of loneliness and fear? Was it a life in which we ignored each other? Thelma wasn't all that different from the day I had arrived. Instead of returning to the real world because of me, she continued to work at getting me to join her in make-believe. Karl remained steadfast and loyal to his organized schedule. I had met many new kids my age, but many of them seemed even more troubled than I was, and they had always had families!

"I'm going to sleep, too," I said. "Good night."

"Good night. See you in the morning," he called, his eyes still following the words on the page of the magazine in his hand.

I went to my room and got ready for bed. After I slipped under the covers, I leaned back on my pillow and reached for the graphs. I knew what I had written on mine, but I didn't know what was on Bernie's.

His numbers were as high as mine, but what he wrote on the bottom drew my interest.

I have never been strongly attracted to anyone this way before. I wonder if this means Crystal is special or if it is a natural reaction to kissing a pretty girl.

Most everyone else, I thought, would think what he wrote was very strange, but I knew this was the only way Bernie could say "I love you."

For now, it would have to do.

I had great hope for tomorrow.

Tonight, for once, it was easy to close my eyes, dream, and fall asleep.

10
Heart's Desire

Ashley looked frightened when I confronted her at school the next day. Bernie had been afraid that she would go around spreading stories about us, but instead, she was afraid we would spread stories about her.

"Did you stay?" she asked me in a whisper when we met at our lockers in the hallway. She checked to be sure no one could over-hear our conversation.

"Yes," I said.

"And did you do it?" she quickly followed.

"Of course," I said, slamming my locker shut and starting for homeroom. She trailed along like a puppy tugged on an invisible leash.

"What happened?" she gasped.

I stopped and spun on her. "If you want to know so much, why didn't you stay?"

"I couldn't," she said, her face looking as if she would break into hysterical sobs any moment.

"Did you tell anyone? Helga, for example?"

She shook her head so vigorously I

thought her eyes would rattle.

"Good," I said, continuing on to home-room. She remained beside me, step for step, until she saw Bernie, and then she lowered her head and went to her seat.

Bernie looked at her and then at me, his eyes full of questions. I indicated it was all right, and he relaxed his shoulders. He didn't speak to me until we were passing to our first class. When he approached, Ashley stepped away again.

"I can't meet you for lunch today," he said. "I promised to help Mr. Friedman set up his equipment."

"Okay," I said quickly.

"Is everything all right?"

"Yes," I replied.

"Then you'll be at my house the same time tonight?"

I paused, and he searched anxiously for the answer in my eyes.

"We'll move on down the chart," he added.

"I'll be there," I said. We walked on to class. At lunch, Ashley couldn't wait to join me.

"Are you going to tell me what happened?" she asked as soon as she put her tray on the table and slipped into the chair beside me.

"We only kissed twice," I remarked, my voice as coldly factual as could be.

"Only two? Why just two?"

"It's hard to explain it to someone who wasn't there," I said, "but it was all very scientific. Nothing bad happened."

She actually looked disappointed. "Did you like kissing him?"

"No. I mean yes. I mean . . . listen, I can't talk about it like this," I said sharply. "It makes it sound dirty."

She nodded as if she understood. "I'm not trying to make fun of you, Crystal. It's different for you and Bernie," she said sadly. "You're both so smart. I felt like I didn't belong there with you two, and I was frightened. If you ever want to tell me anything, I promise I'll listen and keep it all to myself."

I saw that although she couldn't be part of our experiments, she wanted to feel as though she was special, as though she was in on it and had clearance to know top-secret things. Ashley is still a little girl, I told myself. For her, this is all still a game, like "you show me yours, and I'll show you mine." However, if I drove her away, she could turn on us and might spread stories.

"Okay," I promised. "I'll tell you stuff when there's something to tell, when there are real, scientific conclusions."

She smiled. "Can you come over to my house Friday night and have dinner with me and my mother?" she asked. "My father is

164

still away on a business trip," she added before I could ask. From the way she spoke about him, I understood that he was away almost as much as he was there. "Maybe you can help me with my math for the big test next week."

"I'll ask my parents," I promised. She beamed.

I understood that Ashley wasn't very popular and was rarely invited to anything. The other girls treated her as though she was socially below them, an outsider because of her size and timidity. Despite what had occurred at Bernie's house, I was rapidly becoming her best friend. She looked up to me and liked the fact that although the other girls weren't necessarily friendly, they were not anxious to challenge me head on, either. Years of institutionalized life had hardened my outer shell, perhaps. I was certainly unafraid of girls like Helga, back-stabbers who gossiped about you in the girls' room but shut right up when you were face-to-face with them. They had so many misconceptions about orphans. If they wanted to believe I was capable of scratching their eyes out, let them, I thought. Long ago, I learned that if I couldn't have another girl or boy like me for who I was, it was better they feared me. At least then I was safe.

As the school day drew to a close, I felt excitement building inside me like distant thunder on the horizon. Every once in a while, a small jolt of electricity shot through my heart. My stomach sizzled and didn't stop. I could barely eat dinner. How far would we go on Bernie's chart? When I gazed at the pages alone in my room, they felt like fire in my hands. The heat traveled up my arms and swirled around my heart. Looking at myself in the mirror, I saw how flushed my cheeks were and how charged my eyes appeared. Would Karl take one look at me and understand? Would Thelma, whose daily dose of passion through the television set could choke Venus?

"Are you feeling all right tonight, Crystal?" Karl did ask at dinner.

Thelma looked up anxiously.

"Yes," I said. "I'm just a little concerned about my first math exam."

"Oh," Thelma said with a laugh. "You'll probably get a hundred. Won't she, Karl?"

"She'll do well," he agreed. "Being nervous about your tests is all right as long as it doesn't interfere with your performance. It's the students who don't worry about their tests who do the worst. You're a truly self-motivated young lady, Crystal. We're very proud of that, aren't we, Thelma?"

"What? Oh, yes, we are, dear. The other parents are going to be so jealous of us," she added happily. "Your school grades were one of the first things Karl considered, right, Karl?"

"Yes, they were," he admitted.

I gazed at both of them and thought for a moment. If I had received C's instead of A's, they wouldn't have adopted me. It didn't seem right somehow to base so much on test results, certainly not when it came to making someone your daughter. If my grades fell off, would they give me back?

"Ashley Raymond asked me if I would have dinner with her and her mother this Friday," I said. "Would that be all right?"

"Actually," Karl said, "that would be perfect. I don't think we'll be back in time for dinner. I was going to have Thelma prepare something for you to heat up."

"Back in time? Where are we going, Karl?" Thelma sounded confused.

"Don't you remember, Thelma?" he asked softly. "We have an appointment with the doctors and administrator at the clinic concerning your father's condition. He's going to have to be moved to another facility where he can get more round-the-clock attention."

"I hate doing those things," she muttered.

167

"Can't we just phone them?"

"No, dear. There are papers to sign. It won't take that long." He smiled at me. "Thelma doesn't like to remember sad things. With the time it takes to go to the home and back, I didn't want you waiting on us for dinner, Crystal."

"Maybe she can go with us, Karl?"

"You just heard her say Ashley invited her to dinner, Thelma. Let her get to know other children her age," Karl declared. "You want her to have friends, don't you?"

"Yes," she said in a small voice. Ever since her mother's death, she seemed to be even more withdrawn and afraid of real life. I thought if she could crawl right into the television set or into a book, she would.

"That's settled, then," Karl said.

Thelma started to eat again and then stopped.

"You know what's on tonight, Crystal? *Romance Theater*, and it's a brand-new story," she said.

"I'm studying for my math test with Bernie Felder," I said. It wasn't a total lie. I expected Bernie and I were going to do some of that.

"Oh. Well," she said, thinking, "maybe I'll tape it for you to watch with me later this weekend, okay?"

"That would be nice," I said, and she looked satisfied.

Karl stared at me with troubled eyes. I avoided his gaze and finished my dinner. After helping Thelma with the dishes, I went to my room, gathered my books, and stuck our graphs into my notebook. Thelma was already involved in a television program. Karl was settled in his chair, reading the *Wall Street Journal*.

"Don't be too late," he called when I went to the front door.

"I won't." I took a deep breath and went out.

It was a clear evening, the stars looking somehow bigger, brighter. The street was quiet, but the shadows looked deeper and longer, and my heart filled my ears with a thumping so loud I didn't hear any cars go by. When I reached Bernie's front door, I felt as if I had floated to it. My finger trembled against the door button. I heard it ding inside, and moments later, Bernie opened it.

"Hi," he said.

"Hi." I stepped in, half expecting to see his mother, too, but as usual, his house was quiet.

"No one's home," he said quickly, and followed that with a conspiratorial smile. "Don't worry. We're not going to be interrupted."

"I thought we might study a little for the

math test, too," I said.

"Sure, but it's going to be easy. Mr. Albert's first tests always are. He likes to give everyone the feeling they can do well. False hope," he quipped as we walked to his room. As soon as we entered, he closed the door and then turned to me. "Did you bring the graphs back?"

"Yes," I said, taking them out of the notebook and handing them to him.

He gazed down at them as if he had forgotten what was written.

"Good," he said, and looked at me. "Are you ready?" I hesitated, and he looked worried. "You still want to go on with the experiment, don't you?"

"Sure, sure I do." I wanted to tell him how much I'd been thinking about our kisses, but I was afraid he wouldn't want to continue if I wasn't serious about the experiment.

I couldn't help but hope that for Bernie too, our experiment was more than just a scientific test.

Bernie's kiss started off sweet like the first time, but soon he became more insistent, forcing me to kiss him deeper and longer. These sorts of kisses made me nervous, but not in the good, special way I'd felt before. As Bernie pressed his lips and then his body against mine, I couldn't help but feel that he wanted to do more than just kiss.

Pushing him away, I took a step backward.

"Bernie, stop, we need to take breaks to write down our results." I hoped I sounded calm; inside I felt as if my heart would break from beating so quickly.

"Aw, come on, Crystal, it was just starting to get interesting." He stepped toward me and reached out to put his hands on my shoulder.

"Bernie, no, I'm not comfortable with this." I turned away and walked toward his desk. I grabbed my chart and started to write down my results, but my hands were shaking so badly I couldn't do much more than scrawl.

"Crystal, I don't understand. Did I do something wrong? Don't you want to continue with the experiment?" Bernie sounded hurt, and although I knew we had to stop this, I didn't want him to think I didn't like him.

"No, Bernie, it's nothing like that. It's just that . . . this is starting to feel like more than an experiment . . . and I don't think I'm ready for that." I hoped he would appreciate my honesty.

"Well, fine, Crystal. I guess you're just like Ashley . . . too scared to do anything adult, even in the name of science!" He stormed to the bedroom door. "I can't believe you're acting like this is something . . . something wrong or dirty or whatever. You're obviously way younger than I thought. I think you'd better leave, Crystal. And don't bother coming back."

As I ran out of Bernie's house, tears streaming down my face, I couldn't help but feel I was wrong to have ended our experiment. I wanted to be able to return. Bernie was my friend. I didn't mean to make him feel we'd done something dirty. In fact, I was beginning to think there was something special between us, that what we were doing meant something. And I hoped maybe Bernie thought that, too. Now I guess I'd never find out how he really felt about me. If his thoughts were of me when we were kissing . . . or if he was really only thinking of charts and graphs.

Maybe Thelma was right — it was much easier to be involved in someone else's life on TV than it was to be involved in your own real life.

At my house, I stopped and sat on a lawn chair to catch my breath. I didn't want to go inside looking and feeling as I did. They would wonder why I was home so soon, anyway. Before Bernie, I thought, I had never had a boy even try to kiss me.

The night air chilled me. I embraced myself and rocked back and forth. I couldn't throw off the bad feelings.

How hard it was to get someone to love you in a way that made you happy, I thought, but how desperately we wanted it and needed it. Suddenly, Thelma didn't seem as silly and distracted to me as I had believed. She only wanted to be loved as much as the characters on her soap operas were loved.

Karl and Thelma looked up when I entered.

"Home so soon?" Karl asked.

"There wasn't much to study." I gazed at the television set. "So I thought I would come home and watch the program with Mom."

"Really?" she cried.

Karl looked at me suspiciously, his eyes narrowing.

"Everything all right?" he asked.

"Yes."

"Why wouldn't everything be all right?" Thelma demanded. "She's home to watch the show with me. That's all."

She absolutely glowed. Her eyes were bright with happiness.

"Yes," I said. "Yes, I am."

"You're just in time," she said, and made a place for me beside her.

11
Shattered Dreams
🐚

Bernie was waiting by my locker in the morning. I glanced at him and went right to unlocking my combination lock.

"I'm sorry," he said. "I think we just went too fast on the chart. Can't we try again?"

"No. I think we were right yesterday. Let's wait and see what happens naturally." I hoped I sounded more sure of myself than I felt.

"You're the only person I would have ever done this with," he said sadly, turned, and walked away.

Ashley was watching from across the hall. She hurried over to me.

"My parents said I could come to your house for dinner Friday night," I said. Her eyes brightened like Christmas tree lights. "Don't ask me any other questions," I said sharply. "Not a single one."

She took one look at my face and nodded. Bernie wasn't there at lunch, and he avoided looking at me in class. I put all my concentration into my schoolwork, driving every other thought from my mind. Ashley was so afraid of my demeanor, she walked and sat quietly beside me all day, becoming talkative only after the final bell, when we were on our way to the bus.

"I'll tell my mother you're coming. After we eat and study our math, maybe we can listen to some music. I bought two new CDs this week. Do you like Timmy and the Grasshoppers?"

"I never heard of them." I turned to look at her. "I rarely listen to rock music."

"Oh," she said softly.

I sighed deeply. "But maybe I should be brought up to date. Sure," I said. "We'll listen to some music."

"Great."

She bounced ahead of me onto the bus. Bernie was in the rear in his usual seat already. He kept his eyes on his book. I took a seat in the middle, and Ashley got in beside me.

"Aren't you two becoming the cozy ones?" Helga quipped as she walked past.

"Jealous?" I asked with a cold smile.

"Of what?" she shot back, glancing at her friends for the applause she expected in their eyes.

"Of intelligence, personality, charm, wit, in short, everything you're missing," I fired back.

Her mouth opened and closed as she searched for some proper response, but the kids behind her in the aisle shouted for her to move along, and she just twisted her shoulder and tossed back her hair.

"You're not afraid of anyone, are you?" Ashley asked with a voice full of admiration.

I thought. "Yes," I said.

"Who?" she wanted to know.

"Myself," I said.

Of course, I knew she wouldn't understand. It would be years before she would.

The next two days were much the same. I put most of my attention and energy into my schoolwork, my first term paper, my first big set of exams. At night, I took some time to watch television with Thelma, and she and I began to talk about other things. I learned more and more about her own childhood, her dreams and disappointments. Karl looked pleased and came up with the plan for us to take a weekend holiday in Montreal, in Canada, in two weeks. That made Thelma even happier, and I began to believe that maybe we could be a real family after all.

On Friday, after school, I returned home, changed, did some of the schoolwork I wanted out of the way, and then walked over to Ashley's house. Her mother was very happy to see me. I was actually embarrassed by all the attention. No one, not even Thelma, was so attentive, fawned over me so much, and worried that I wouldn't like what she was preparing for dinner, concerned that she had what I liked to drink and what I liked for dessert.

"How often is your father away like this?" I asked Ashley when we were alone in her room after dinner. The empty chair at the head of the table was conspicuous. It gave me an eerie feeling, as if a ghost were sitting there. Whether out of habit or just to keep the table looking balanced, Ashley's mother placed a setting at the head of the table.

"Almost every other week these days. They fight a lot about it," Ashley revealed. "Last week, my mother accused him of having another family."

"Does he have to work like that?"

"He says he does," she replied sadly. "I feel sorry for her. She's alone so much."

I nodded sympathetically. So many of the kids I had met in school who had families were just as lonely as I had been. In various ways, their homes and lives were shattered and held together by the weakest glue, and although they didn't live in an institutional setting as I had, they often wore the faces of orphans, faces that revealed their loneliness, a longing for more affection and love, their eyes searching the faces of their friends, looking to see if anyone had more.

I went to Ashley's math book and helped her understand our newest assignments. She seemed to understand.

"You should be a teacher," she said. "You're better than Mr. Albert."

"Hardly." I laughed.

We were about to listen to music when we heard the phone ring. Ashley paused. I could see she was hoping it was her father calling from wherever he was. She was practically holding her breath. That was why we both heard her mother cry out so clearly.

"Oh, no! When?" she screamed.

Ashley's eyes were flooded quickly with fear. Moments later, her mother came to the door of Ashley's bedroom. I glanced at Ashley's face. She was nearly in tears, anticipating the worst.

"Crystal," Mrs. Raymond said, turning to me instead. "There's been a terrible accident. Do you know your uncle Stuart's number in Albany?"

"I'm sure it's in my father's Rolodex," I said. "I'll go look it up." I ran from the room before she could tell me another thing. My heart was pounding so hard that my legs felt like rubber. I nearly tripped at the front door. Outside, I broke into a trot. Tears were already blurring my vision. What sort of an accident? What did it mean?

I charged into my house and down the hall to Karl's den. After I found Uncle Stuart's telephone number, I took a deep breath, unable to swallow down a lump in my throat that threatened to choke off my air.

Nevertheless, I ran out again and back to Ashley's house. I went in and thrust the telephone number at her mother as if I were a relay runner passing the wand. She took it slowly, her eyes on me, filled with tears. She told us she'd explain after she'd talked with Uncle Stuart and asked us to wait in the living room. I left the room with Ashley but lingered outside in the hall. I just couldn't wait any longer to hear what had happened.

Ashley looked scared but moved down the hallway to be near me. We looked at each other and then turned as Mrs. Raymond began to speak.

"Stuart," she said, "this is Vera Raymond, Thelma's friend. Yes, yes, I'm fine. Stuart, a friend of my husband's in the police department here just called me. There's been a terrible accident. A car accident. Karl and Thelma . . . both of them have been killed, Stuart. I'm so sorry," she said.

Ashley stifled a cry with her fist in her

mouth. I shook my head at her.

No, that's not true, I thought. Karl's too good a driver. He's the most careful driver in the world. They're too young to die.

"Yes, it happened today, just a few hours ago. A drunk driver in a pickup truck crossed the median to their side of the highway. They had no chance. I'm sorry."

Pickup truck? A drunk driver? For a moment, it was like eavesdropping on someone else's life. I felt I was watching and listening to one of Thelma's shows. It was make-believe, fantasy, some serial show. Boy, is Thelma going to be angry about this one, I thought. Just when she got so attached to the characters, they write them out of the show. I shook my head.

Ashley was staring at me in the strangest way. She looked frozen in time, a wax figure of fear.

"Yes," Mrs. Raymond said quietly. "She's with us. What do you want to do?"

There was a silence, and my mind raced with what Stuart could be telling her. What would happen to me? Would I be sent back to the orphanage?

"I understand, Stuart, but what do you want me to do in the interim? Really? All right. I'll find out and take care of it," she said. "I'm very sorry, Stuart. It's hit me so hard, I'm having trouble absorbing it myself. I'm sorry."

She hung up and slowly walked out into the hallway. From the look on her face, I could tell that she was startled to see me standing there but also a little relieved that she didn't have to explain the tragedy all over again.

"I'm sorry, Crystal," she said. "It's so horrible. I'm sorry, honey."

"I've got to go home now," I said. "I promised my mother I wouldn't stay out too late. They like me to be there when they return."

"No, honey, listen to me."

"Thank you so much for dinner, Mrs. Raymond. Thanks, Ashley. I'll call you. Thanks," I said, and rushed to the door.

"Crystal!" Mrs. Raymond shouted, but I was out the door again, running hard this time until I was gasping for breath at my front door. I charged through and shouted.

"I'm home!"

The silence greeted me. It was like being in Bernie's house. I stood there with my hand on my side, breathing hard, listening.

That was just some show, I kept telling myself. Ashley's mother is like Thelma. She loves her shows, too. I bet I know which one it was, I thought. I laughed. Sure, I told myself, I bet I know.

When the doorbell rang, I was sitting in Thelma's chair watching television. I ignored it, and it rang again and again. Someone started to pound on it. A voice threatened to break it down. The doorbell rang again. There was more pounding. When the commercial came on, I rose and went to the door.

A man and a woman were standing there. The man was in a suit and tie. He wore glasses and carried a small briefcase. The woman was short and wide in the hips. She had dark brown hair cut in a short, straight style. I could smell the child welfare agency on them. They had the look.

"Hello, Crystal. My name's Mr. Kolton, and this is Ms. Thacker. We're here to help you," he said.

"I can't go anywhere yet," I said. "My show is still on."

"What?" he asked.

"I'm watching something on television, something Thelma would watch and want to know about later when she returns. She forgot to set up the video recorder."

They looked at each other, and the woman shook her head.

"You're going to be all right," the man said with an institutional smile. To me, it looked as if they were both wearing familiar masks, masks I had seen all my life.

"I don't know that yet," I said. "We have to wait for the ending."

I left them standing in the doorway and returned to the television set. They came in. The woman sat with me while the man made some calls. A few hours later, I was in the rear of their car, heading back to the lair of the monster, the system, the only real mother and father I had ever known.

Epilogue

"This is going to be a lot better than the orphanage, Crystal," Ms. Thacker promised as we approached the driveway of the Lakewood House.

Ahead of us was a very large two-story house of gray clapboard with a wraparound porch. There were maple and weeping willow trees in front and lots of green lawn. As we drew closer, I saw there was a lake in the rear.

"Louise Tooey is probably the best foster mother we have. She treats all her wards as though they were her very own children. All of them say so," Ms. Thacker continued.

"This actually was once a resort," Mr. Kolton added. "And a very popular one at that. There's a rather big dining room, a nice lobby, ballfields."

"Beautiful grounds," Ms. Thacker emphasized.

"Maybe you would like to move in with me," I said dryly.

She just glanced at me and then smiled

with that syrupy look of understanding I hated and continued to look out the window.

"There are other girls your age here, and the school system you'll attend is one of the best," Mr. Kolton said.

"How do you know that?" I queried. He glanced back at me and kept driving without replying.

"Crystal does well wherever she goes to school," Ms. Thacker said. Mr. Kolton laughed. "She'll probably end up tutoring the other kids here, won't you, Crystal?"

I didn't reply. I stared out the window, but I wasn't looking at my new home. My thoughts were back at the funeral I had just attended. Ironically, Karl had been right in planning it all before his and Thelma's deaths. The agency had decided I could attend the service even though Karl and Thelma had not completed the adoption process. Their family members all offered me their condolences and then guiltily explained that they had no place for me. Karl's brothers couldn't take me in. His father and Thelma's father were incapable of being guardians, and Thelma had no relatives who were interested.

Ashley and her mother were at the funeral, as were Uncle Stuart and some people from

Karl's office. Before the ceremony ended, I looked back and saw Bernie standing near a tree, watching. After the final prayers were said, I headed toward the car with Mr. Kolton and Ms. Thacker. Ashley ran up to hug me and to promise she would write me if I would write her. I nodded. I hated promises. They were like those balloons I had seen drifting in the wind. They had shape until the air escaped, and then everyone forgot them.

Bernie stepped out from the tree, and I stopped.

"I thought you didn't approve of funerals," I said.

"I don't, but I wanted to be here for you."

"What's that, step seven?" I asked.

He looked down.

"I'm sorry," I said. He looked up at me. "We were both wrong. We both should have just said what we felt and not used any disguises."

He nodded.

"I guess we did learn something important, then," he said.

"Yes. I guess we did."

I got into the car. He stood there and waved as we drove off.

I could still see him standing there now. I blinked and woke to the present as Mr.

Kolton brought the car to a stop in front of the big house. They got out my things, and we walked inside. A boy and a girl, not older than ten or eleven, were playing a board game on a big table. They looked up with curiosity. A door opened at the rear of the hall, and a tall woman with her shoulder-length brown hair swinging loosely about her face came hurrying out to greet us. Although she had a pretty face and bright blue eyes, the wrinkles in her forehead and at the corners of her eyes were deep enough to cause me to think she was older than she first appeared.

"Hello," she cried with excitement. "I was in the kitchen and didn't hear you drive up. I suppose this is Crystal. Hi, Crystal. Welcome to the Lakewood. This is going to be a real home. You'll see. You have a nice roommate, too. Her name is Janet, and she's the sweetest little girl. She's shy, but I bet you'll get her to be more outgoing. They tell me you're very smart," she said. "We sure could use some help in that department," she told Mr. Kolton. He smiled. I thought she would never stop talking. "Although my kids usually do well. We insist they do their homework before anything else. There are rules here, but good rules. Oh, I forgot to introduce myself. I'm Louise Tooey," she said,

187

holding out her hand.

I took it to shake, but she held onto mine and patted it.

"I know you're a little frightened about being in a new place, but this is a special place. It was once one of the most popular tourist houses. It's really a very warm place, full of fun. You'll see. Anyway . . ."

"Go on!" we heard someone shout.

A boy about fourteen came charging down the stairway. His face was full of fear. Above him, a tall man with a wooden face towered above us all. He had thick shoulders and long, muscular arms, one of which had a tattoo on the forearm.

"Gordon," Louise said, nodding at Mr. Kolton and Ms. Thacker. "The agency is here with a new girl."

His threatening posture relaxed, and the face that had looked so dangerous moments before softened.

"Well, hello there," he said. He glanced at the boy. "Go on and do your chores, Billy," he said sternly. Then he smiled at Mr. Kolton. "Got to maintain discipline around here."

"Of course," Mr. Kolton said. The boy hurried out of the building.

"This is Crystal. Crystal, this is my husband, Gordon."

"Welcome," Gordon said. There was something in his eyes that frightened me, an animal look. I glanced at Mr. Kolton and Ms. Thacker to see if they saw it, too, but they seemed oblivious to everything but the task at hand, which was to hand me over and leave.

"Why don't I show Crystal her room and have her meet Janet? Gordon, you can take her suitcases, right?"

"Sure," he said, practically seizing them.

"We'll just be a minute," she told Mr. Kolton.

"Fine. Good luck, Crystal," he called to me as I started for the steps.

"Yes, good luck, honey." Ms. Thacker followed. I didn't look back.

Louise talked a continuous stream as we ascended, describing the house, its history, and how much she enjoyed having foster children.

"You're all precious to us, right, Gordon?" she said.

"Yeah," he muttered. "Precious."

She paused at a door and knocked before opening it. A small girl with a face as perfect as a cherub looked up at us. She lay curled up on her bed. She wore what looked like a tutu and a pair of pointe shoes.

"Janet, you're not sick again, are you,

dear?" Louise asked quickly.

She shook her head.

"Just tired from practicing your ballet?"

She nodded, her eyes on me and full of terror.

"This is your new roommate, Crystal. Crystal, this is Janet. I just know you two will get along well. Janet's not a bad student, either, are you, Janet?"

She shook her head.

"Maybe now that you have a roommate, you won't stay to yourself so much," Louise said.

Gordon slapped the suitcases on the floor. "I got things to do," he grunted.

"Fine, dear," Louise said.

"Yeah, fine," he muttered.

"Gordon growls a lot," Louise said when he left, "but he's a pussycat at heart. Well, I'm going to let you two get acquainted while I go down and finish up the business with the agency people. Feel free to roam about and explore your new home," Louise added. "Welcome again, dear," she said, and left us.

I looked at Janet. She seemed so fragile, but her legs did look firm and muscular.

"You study ballet?" I asked. She nodded.

She's as shy as a butterfly, I thought, and went to my suitcases. She watched me for a few moments and then sat up.

"I don't study it anymore. I don't have any teacher," she said.

I looked back at her. "If you like doing it, just keep doing it. Maybe someday you'll get another teacher," I said.

She smiled. It was a pretty smile, a smile hungry to shine on someone who would give her love. I liked her. Maybe it was good that she was so shy and fragile. Maybe it was good that I would have someone else to look after besides myself, I thought.

I went to the window and looked out toward the lake. "It is pretty here," I said.

In the falling, purplish light of the failing day, the stars began to emerge, each like the tip of a magic wand, full of promises.

Janet and I sat by the window and looked up. I was pleasantly surprised when her hand found mine. We sat silently for a moment. Maybe there wasn't a family out there waiting for us. Maybe the only family we would have was each other. Maybe the only promises we would fulfill were the promises we made to each other. We had no wealth, no currency, nothing to offer each other but trust.

Afterward, she showed me pictures of herself in a ballet costume and began to tell me about her life. It didn't come fast. She had been wounded in love as I had, and she was afraid to confide in anyone. The secrets of our hearts would have to be unraveled like a ball of string, a little at a time. We would weave our pasts, our pains, and our dreams around each other until we were safely in each other's cocoon.

Only then could we go back into the world.